Skin Walkers: Mason

By
Susan Bliler

www.susanbliler.com

ACKNOWLEDGMENTS

Cover fonts, spine, and back cover done by:
Susan Bliler

Editing done by:
Dr. S. Lewis

A big thanks to this round of Beta readers:
Cindy "MoFo Jonez" Hubbard
Abril Rivera Kinter
&
Lynn Braybrook.

Thank you for reading for me, ladies!

Dedication

Carissa Blackbird
Mona "Topo" Poitra
Cindy "Mofo" Hubbard

Thank you, ladies, for all you did for Uncle the last few years of
his life.
The pack will never forget.

Rest in Peace, Richard "Tito" Blackbird.
We love and miss you, Uncle.
"And another thing…"

Chapter 1

It hurt! Aww, God, it hurt! Holding her arm close to her chest, Amanda hurried away from the bustling commons area, hidden behind the towering four-story StoneCrow manor. Zigzagging in near knee-deep snow to the parking lot, she jammed a gloved hand into her coat pocket and fumbled for her keys.

Replaying what had just happened in her head, she struggled to figure out what she'd done wrong. One second she'd been leaving the bonfire being held in the communal area and the next, Mason had her arm wrenched backwards as he sneered down at her.

What had she said? What had she done?

Replaying the scene over and over, she couldn't come up with a single reason for Mason's....*attack*. And an attack, was what it had been.

Amanda had been leaning forward on a horseshoe shaped bench. Arms wrapped around herself, her gloved hands were squeezing her biceps to try and get her circulation going. She and Lilly Mulholland were laughing at a story Cindy KillsPrettyEnemy was telling. Next to Cindy and Lilly, their mates, RedKnife and King, smirked at the tale while on Amanda's left, Mason stared distractedly into the fire with a distant look on his handsome face.

And he was handsome, beautiful almost—in the way that sharks were beautiful. With a commanding presence, Mason EnemyHunter exuded power. His strong jawline was always clean-shaven, his nails always perfectly manicured. He wore his crisp business suits like they were suits of armor, seemingly impenetrable, and he never failed to make Amanda feel dowdy and underdressed in comparison. No matter the situation, Mason always appeared to be in his element. Even sitting at a bonfire alongside BDU-clad Sentries and bundled-up human women, there wasn't a single wisp of Mason's soft pecan-colored hair out of place. It was combed back, styled perfectly in a manner that Amanda envied as she lifted a gloved hand to try to trap her long ebony locks as they billowed in a gust of arctic wind.

Watching Mason out of the corner of her eye, Amanda wondered what had his mind so enraptured. It was obvious he was only half listening to Cindy's story, if at all. Piercing sea-green eyes narrowed in on the flames but didn't blink as his jaw ticked. He was deep in thought. It was obvious by the way everyone laughed at the punchline of Cindy's story while Mason's gaze merely sharpened on the crackling fire. His jaw bunched and flexed and Amanda ached to know what he was thinking, but she didn't ask because she didn't know Mason. Yeah, she'd seen him around the estate and knew he was StoneCrow's Chief Financial Officer, in charge of managing the estate's finances and handling all the bookkeeping, but she'd never officially met him. She wanted to but didn't dare. She'd only just decided to break up with Remy McCabe, and StoneCrow Estates was too small and close-knit of a community for her to try to move on with any of the other Skin Walkers who called it home.

Skin Walkers. Even after years of knowing them, being around them, even dating one of them, she was still awed by their existence. They were shapeshifters, creatures only heard of in mythology or cheesy scary movies, but the Skin Walkers at StoneCrow were very real. They were keepers of these mountains, protectors of the wildlife, defenders of all. It's why she'd been so surprised by Mason's actions. It wasn't typical Skin Walker behavior. In fact, it was the polar opposite. Skin Walkers didn't hurt women or children, ever! It was unheard of and left her in shock. She hadn't been the only one surprised by his behavior either. Cindy and Lilly had been just as stunned by Mason's actions. As Amanda had backed fearfully away from the melee that was a half-dozen Skin Walker Sentries rushing Mason, she'd heard Cindy and Lilly demanding to know "what his problem was."

Now, pulling her truck up in front of her cabin, Amanda's arm was screaming for medical attention. She didn't live at StoneCrow Estates. Her life in the Highwood Mountains pre-dated the erection of StoneCrow Manor and the arrival of the Skin Walkers. It's how she'd met them. Skin Walker Dominant, Monroe StoneCrow, had sent scouts to survey the land for any potential issues. She was their closest neighbor and didn't understand their frequent visits back then, but knew now they'd been vetting her. Apparently, she'd passed muster. Monroe had even offered her residence at his compound, but she'd opted to remain in her cabin just a few short miles down the road from their sprawling estate.

At the moment, she regretted that decision. There was a state-of-the-art medical facility back at StoneCrow boasting some of the finest physicians in the country, but Amanda had been so afraid of what she'd done to elicit Mason's ire that she'd run home like the little coward that she was.

Inside her small cabin, she winced as she shimmied out of her coat, stopping after to rub at the pain throbbing in her arm. Toeing off her snow-covered boots, she padded in her purple thermal socks to the bathroom and flicked on the light before gingerly pulling down the collar of her sweater to look at her shoulder. There was no visible mark, so she tried to push up her sleeve to inspect her elbow, but it hurt too much. Aborting the effort, she set about wrestling a couple of logs onto the embers still smoldering in the wide hearth in her living room. Unlike StoneCrow Manor or the cabins on the Estate grounds, Amanda's cabin wasn't equipped with natural gas or even propane. She had to rely on old fashion heat provided by firewood that she chopped and stacked herself. In a pinch, she'd turn on the electric heaters she had in each room but did so rarely because the electrical bill would sky-rocket. A high electric bill seemed imminent from the difficulty she was having getting the large logs into the hearth with just one hand.

By the time she got one log into place, she was sweating and sucking back tears. She'd gotten pissed and forced her bad arm to help lift the log and now she was paying for it. Fuck, it hurt!

Lowering herself to the rug in front of the fire, she pressed her shoulders into the soft cotton of the sofa behind her. Pulling her cell phone out of her bra, she glared at the screen. It wasn't late, just a little past five, but daylight savings time had just ended, so it was already pitch-black out. Amanda didn't like driving at night, she never had, but there was no way she was going to get an ounce of sleep with the agony coursing through her.

Blowing out a pent-up breath that sent dark strands of hair lifting out of her eyes, she fisted her phone and shoved to her feet. Quickly, she made the rounds to each of her rooms and set all her electric heaters to the lowest setting so the cabin would be warm by the time she got back. If the roads were good, it'd be a fifty-minute drive just to get to the city. All the walk-in clinics would be closed by the time she got to Great Falls, which meant a costly visit to the emergency room.

Great! Just great!

She couldn't afford a medical bill right now, as it was, she'd be lucky if her old-ass Dodge Ram made it to town. Her rig had been acting up lately, but she just didn't have the money to take it to a shop.

Snatching her keys off the hook by the front door, she hit the auto-start button so the vehicle could re-heat while she peed. In a few short minutes, her boots were back on her feet, she'd struggled back into her coat, then grabbed her purse before she was hustling back out the door.

It was going to be a long cold drive, followed by a long wait and then expensive visit in the E.R. tonight, and it was all Mason EnemyHunter's fault!

Chapter 2

Sitting in a plush chair in Dominant Skin Walker Monroe StoneCrow's office, Mason didn't know what had come over him. He was still dazed. One minute, he'd been staring into the dancing flames of the giant bonfire lost in his thoughts when someone had grabbed him. No, not grabbed. That human woman, Amanda, had absently placed her hand on his leg to help herself rise from the seat beside him. It had been a casual gesture, something that would have been commonplace among a group of friends such as those seated on her opposite side, but Mason wasn't her friend. He'd acted instinctively. In a flash and with testament to his animal speed, he had her arm wrenched backwards. Snarling down at her, he'd behaved abhorrently. Once he'd realized his mistake, he'd released her instantly, but it was too late. The bitter scent of her fear followed by the acrid explosion of pain still stung his nostrils and had guilt searing through him.

He'd fucked up, and he'd done so in front of Cindy and RedKnife KillsPrettyEnemy and Lilly and King Mulholland. In a flash, RedKnife and King were on their feet and rushing him. He couldn't blame them.

I attacked a woman.

Still in shock, he shook his head morosely. He needed to get it together. He was getting worse, growing more and more distracted, and if he'd worried over the past few months if anyone noticed, he knew now there'd be some explaining to do for sure.

The door to Monroe's office opened and in strolled the Dominant. A smirk on his lips, eerie crystalline blue eyes, sharp as a hawk's, narrowed on Mason as Monroe bit into a crisp apple and slowly shook his head in clear disapproval.

Speaking around his bite of food, Monroe drawled, "Heard you lost your cool and attacked little Ms. Chandler."

It wasn't a question, so Mason didn't respond.

Circling his desk, Monroe used one hand to unbutton his black suit coat before swallowing his bite of food and sitting.

Mason followed Monroe with his eyes and waited. He knew Monroe well enough to know the little barb wouldn't be the end of it.

The two men were compared to each other often. Mason wasn't sure if it was because they dressed similarly or because they were both renowned for their ruthless business practices. Their looks weren't far off from each other either. Same sleek hairstyle, they also shared the same rugged good looks. But where Monroe's eyes were icy blue, Mason's were deep green. Where Monroe's hair was black as a raven's wing, Mason's was a soft pecan brown. Both favored a clean-shaven jaw and lip, but their accents differed, as well as their mannerisms. Monroe had been born and raised in America, while Mason had been raised in England and hadn't lost the hint of his accent even after all the years he'd been in the U.S.

Tossing his half-eaten apple into the trash, Monroe placed his elbows on his desk, lacing his fingers together before leaning forward, his eyes intent on Mason. "Stop fucking staring and explain yourself," Monroe demanded.

Heaving a little sigh, Mason lifted a thumb and pressed it into his bottom lip a moment before dropping it. "I was distracted."

Unclasping his hands, Monroe sat up straight, his mouth rounding in a silent and mocking 'O'. "Her again?"

It irked Mason because he knew that Monroe knew good and god damn well what had happened. Lately, Mason's preoccupation was causing little...slip-ups. This, however, was the first time a human or a female had paid the price.

Leaning back in his chair, Monroe rubbed the pad of his thumb against his fingertips while he stared at Mason.

Mason hated that look because it wasn't ever the casual perusal that Monroe played it off to be. It was a penetrating assessment. Mason could feel Monroe weighing whether or not he was a liability. No doubt, Monroe was inwardly deciding whether or not Mason was worth these little spurts of inconvenience.

"It won't happen again," Mason gritted out.

Without blinking, Monroe countered, "You said that last time."

"That was different," Mason fumed. "That was an accounting error that..."

"Cost me thousands of dollars," Monroe filled in. "Whereas this," he left the sentence open-ended and stared pointedly at Mason, allowing him to finish.

Reluctantly, Mason lowered his head. "Was a highly unacceptable show of dominance against a human female who wasn't expecting it and couldn't have prevented it or protected herself from it even if she'd wanted to."

An explosive sigh filled the air, as Monroe's stony mask slipped. "It's been six years, Mason. Maybe it's time we start considering the possibility that she might be...*gone*."

The words pissed Mason off. Mostly because he'd been thinking the same thing himself as of late and it never failed to produce an unacceptable amount of guilt. Still, he raged, "If you were in my shoes, what would you do? Would you just stop looking? Would you just give up?"

Jaw ticking once, Monroe's eyes went hard. "I *don't* give up."

Satisfied that Monroe was at least honest, Mason sat back in his chair. "I'll do better. I'll schedule an hour or two after my shift to dedicate solely to the task. I won't allow my personal business to filter into the rest of my day. I'll be more focused."

"And you'll apologize to Amanda Chandler."

"I'll apologize to Amanda," Mason agreed.

"You'll have to deal with Remy too. They're seeing each other."

Chuffing a humorless sound, Mason rolled his eyes. "I'm not worried about Remy *fucking* McCabe."

"I'm just letting you know that she's his."

And that pissed Mason off too. "If she were his, he would have been sitting next to her at the bonfire. She's always showing up to these Walker events, her sad little eyes always seeking him out, and he's always a no-show. He's a piece of shit who took advantage of a beautiful and lonely woman. She's not his Angel. She's not his anything."

Monroe's brows winged up at Mason's outburst, but Mason couldn't stop himself now that he'd started, finally finding a fitting outlet for his anger.

"That pretty little punk can come see me if he has issue with *my* mistake. I'll gladly make amends with Amanda, but I don't owe Remy shit." He shoved up out of his chair. "And if he dares to come around playing the valiant hero, I'll put him on his ass."

Knowing better than to just storm out, regardless of how much he wanted to, Mason gritted out, "Again, I apologize for my actions. I'll make things right with Ms. Chandler. It will never happen again."

Monroe was studying him intently, his eyes sparking with some known emotion before he jerked his chin once toward the door by way of dismissal. "See that it doesn't."

Mason left Monroe's office annoyed that he felt like a delinquent who'd been summoned to the principal's office. It was happening too often lately and making him look not only unprofessional but foolish as well. Worse, there was no one to blame but himself. He needed to get his shit together. He also needed to speak with Conn Drago. Sending Conn and his team of mercenaries out hunting during the work week was going to have to change too because Mason simply couldn't focus when his head and heart were too preoccupied by stupid hope. Hope that never ceased to be demolished under the crushing heel of failure.

First things first, though. Right now, he needed to find Amanda Chandler and apologize. It was a task he wasn't looking forward to because there was really no excuse that was acceptable. He was a trained Skin Walker Sentry, a stage five Walker, who had no right or reason to ever mishandle a female, ever!

Chapter 3

Everything was impossible. Growling in frustration, Amanda wished she could have just stayed in bed as she kicked open her front door and stomped in booted feet out onto her snow-covered porch. She'd been stuck in Great Falls for hours last night and hadn't returned until after midnight. X-rays had shown that her forearm had a hairline fracture, and a tendon in her shoulder had also been torn. It'd been hard refusing to take the pain meds the physician had offered her at the hospital, but knowing she had to drive herself back to the mountains prevented her from taking anything until she'd gotten home. Luckily, the pain meds she'd been prescribed had put her down for the rest of the night.

Standing on the porch feeling a little groggy and with her arm in a sling, she frowned at all the snow that had piled up outside. She hadn't gotten the chance to shovel yesterday so her feet sunk into the knee-deep snow drift that had buried her front steps. All morning, she'd been working on chores in the house and everything had taken so much longer than it normally would have, so much so that she was well behind schedule. She'd intended on doing at least some work last night after she'd returned from the clinic in town, but after she'd downed the pain pills, she'd passed out trying to process all that had happened.

Now, good and pissed and ready to tackle the impossible task of shoveling a path to the side of her cabin and clearing out a space so she could split some much-needed firewood, she heaved a weighty sigh that left her feeling a little light-headed. How she was going to pull this off with one arm and feeling hung-over from the pain meds, she had no idea; but living out here all alone meant there was no other choice.

Stumbling down the snow-covered steps, she ignored the sharp bite of winter chill that blasted her skin. She'd worked up a sweat inside that still clung to her skin beneath the sweater she wore. A sweater that had taken her twenty minutes to get into because of her arm. Earlier, she'd wanted to change out of it, but knowing how much effort it would take, she opted to keep that sucker on.

Eyeing her front yard, she noted the pristine blanket of untouched snow that covered everything. The mountain had dumped two feet of snow overnight and it'd be beautiful if it didn't mean hours of struggle for her.

Gaze shifting to her old pick-up, Amanda cringed at how foolish it had been to not plug in the head bolt heater when she'd gotten home last night. It'd be a bitch to start today, if it started at all, and there was no one to blame for that except her lazy-ass self.

And Mason fucking EnemyHunter!

She'd been stewing over his behavior all morning. It was the first thing she'd thought about when she woke. Well...second after the pain in her shoulder. She'd been so pissed and her ire only grew with each passing second until she'd decided, about an hour ago, that she was going to send him her medical bill once it arrived. He should have to pay for the damage he'd done because after going over the whole incident about a million times, Amanda knew she hadn't done anything wrong. Part of her even wanted to contact Remy to let him know what had happened. Yeah, it'd be in bad form to try and get her soon-to-be-ex to beat up Mason for tweaking her arm, but fuck! It still hurt and that ass, Mason, deserved a little of his own medicine. It wouldn't happen though because for as mighty as Amanda was in her head, she was a coward in reality, which meant there'd be no way she'd ever actually send Mason her doctor's bill. She also wouldn't be contacting Remy. She knew he'd defend her to Mason if she asked, but she wouldn't ask because she didn't want to talk to Remy. Things between them had grown awkward and she'd only just found the courage to start attending StoneCrow events alone. She didn't need Remy racing back into her life when it was clearly some place he didn't want to be.

Struggling her way through the deep snow to circle the house, Amanda was relieved to find that the snow at the back of the cabin was just a light dusting on the ground thanks to the buffer from the house. She kept her cords of wood stacked up here for that very reason, knowing the snow tended to drift against the front of the cabin while the back was typically blocked. She'd also built an overhang back here to keep the snow from covering her precious fuel source.

In faded jeans and a rose-colored sweater over a pair of Cuddl Duds, she was glad for the layers as the snow melted against her jeans. Wool socks and her tall winter boots covered her feet, but it didn't take long for the sharp bite of wind to cut through her like a knife. Left arm in a sling, she eyed the axe opting to start here rather than with shoveling because it was important for her to prioritize right now. If she could only get through one outdoor chore today, it needed to be prepping firewood. Shoveling could wait.

Using her good hand, she gripped the axe handle from where the tool rested on a chopping block. Rocking it back and forth, she pulled it free. In about three swings, she knew she'd be warmed up again, but three swings were easier said than done. Hell, she struggled just to get a piece of wood off the tall cord stacked high against the house and had just as much trouble positioning it on the chopping block. Her hands were small so there was no hope of handling the wood by simply grabbing one end like Remy could do, and her other arm was practically useless so she had to roll the wood up the front of her body and use her good arm to press it firmly against her stomach just to get it where she wanted it. It pissed her off when the bark snagged her sweater. This was one of her favorite sweaters, *goddamnit!*

Heaving an exasperated sigh when the log was finally settled, Amanda took a moment to pull at the snag in the front of her sweater wondering if she could fix it later. The thought was aborted when she realized it'd take a great deal more damage before her work was done. Offering a frown for the loss, she gripped the handle of her ax with her good hand and glared at the wood. This wasn't going to work. There was no way... Before she could talk herself out of it, she sucked in a breath and threw all of her weight into hefting the ax into a wide arc. She knew before it even connected that it wasn't going to split the log, and it didn't. With a dull thud, the axe buried itself maybe an inch or two into the top of the wood.

With a quietly muttered, *"Shhhit!"* she walked up and clamped the log between her knees to hold it in place while wiggling the ax handle back and forth until it pried free. This was going to take forever.

Chapter 4

In hawk form, Mason watched Amanda from where he was perched in the cover of the trees surrounding her property. Her little homestead was quaint yet efficient. The property set-up had clearly been well thought out, and he couldn't help but wonder if that was her doing or if someone else was responsible. Lifting his beak again, he scented the air and found no trace of a male scent. Hawk form wasn't the best for sniffing out scents, but it was great for watching and watching was all he wanted to do.

Amanda Chandler.

He said her name in his head for the hundredth time since the bonfire incident and mentally went over all he'd learned about her in the past twenty-four hours. She was thirty-four, just three years younger than him. She was supposedly Remy McCabe's girlfriend, which he already knew, but he also knew that Remy had been avoiding the poor woman for weeks. It happened often when Skin Walkers attached themselves to a woman who wasn't their Angel.

Angels were sacred. They were rare. It was easy for Skin Walkers to know once they'd met their one true mate because the affliction hit hard and fast. *Affliction.* Studying Amanda, Mason thought on the phenomena that hit Walker males like a sledgehammer to the nuts. At least that's how he'd heard other Walkers describe it. He himself had yet to find his Angel and wasn't currently looking. He had more pressing matters at hand than indulging his own imperative need for his One. And it would be imperative. Affliction would not and could not be ignored. Not even by the strongest of them. Preoccupied with the need to collar and claim their mate, the afflicted Skin Walker would forego eating, drinking, and sleeping until the claiming was complete. No, forego wasn't the right word. Forego implied they could indulge in the life sustaining trinity, but they couldn't. During the affliction it was physically impossible for a Walker to eat, drink, or sleep. It was nature's way of forcing a mating, ensuring that Walker wasn't too blind or proud to overlook the Creator's gift. Much like a rutting bull elk, urged by his desire to ensure that his seed is passed on, Walker males would fight anyone to claim their

Angel and then fight to keep her. It was to ensure that the seed of only the strongest and most virile of their species was passed on, and it was during this affliction that Walkers were at their most volatile.

Canting his head, he watched as wisps of black hair with blue undertones that reminded him of midnight licked around Amanda's face. The wind was harsh, and she wasn't wearing a coat, but he couldn't imagine how she'd manage the feat with the sling that held her injured arm.

She'd been living out here alone when Monroe had purchased his acreage just a few miles up the road from her. After years of investing and watching, Monroe had deemed her a "non-threat" and had allowed her to remain on the mountain. Mason knew from past experience that there wasn't any price Monroe wouldn't pay to buy off property of those living in these mountains that he deemed a threat to Walker kind. Amanda wasn't one of those, so she stayed, and had become friends with several of the women at the Estate...as well as forging a relationship with Remy.

Eyes scanning the tree-line, Mason sought out any evidence that Remy had been here recently. *Someone* had been. With his keen animal eyesight, he picked up large footprints in the snow, but they only skirted the perimeter of Amanda's property, never coming any closer than a few hundred feet. *Odd.* Why would Remy be spying on his girlfriend?

From what Mason had learned, Amanda and Remy had been dating for four months. It was an on and off relationship that had turned mostly off lately. If rumors were true, Amanda intended to end things with Remy. He smirked at that. Remy was well known at StoneCrow as a lady's man, and Mason knew it would be a blow to the Walker Sentry's ego to be dismissed, especially by a human female. Maybe that's why Remy was slinking around. He was probably trying to find a way back into Ms. Chandler's heart.

Amanda's hissed, "Shhhhit," drew his attention back to her.

He watched as she used a booted foot and her good arm to pry her axe free from the log she'd failed to split. Splitting wood would be difficult for a woman in peak physical condition, so watching Amanda struggle at the task knowing it was his fault she was having such a hard time filled him with guilt.

Eyes locked on Amanda, they narrowed when she cursed some more and then ripped the sling from around her neck. Gingerly removing it from her injured arm, she tossed the sling into the snow and then, to Mason's shock, she gripped the axe handle with both hands.

Surely, she's not going to...

A wince claimed her delicate features an instant before she lifted the axe and steadied it in front of her with both hands.

Son of a bitch!

Mason dove from his branch and shot straight for Amanda, but it was too late. Before he could get to her, she was swinging the axe up and over her head with a pain-filled grunt. In a blink and with a jarring thud, the axe buried about six inches into the log and then toppled to the side as Amanda screamed and released the handle. Falling to her knees, her hand shot up to her injured shoulder and clamped onto it in a white-knuckled grip. Eyes pinched shut, Amanda Lamaze-breathed through the pain that

Mason could scent before he even landed. It was intense and unpleasant and had his animals stirring within him even as a wave of agitation crashed over him. He shoved it back as he sailed toward her.

She must have caught his movement because tear-soaked eyes lifted and locked on him, and motherfucker! This was the second time in a twenty-four hour span that she'd stared at him in clear agony. Agony he'd caused whether directly or indirectly.

Gliding low, he shifted before he landed. Clad in dark jeans and a charcoal sweater, he slid on one knee, using a booted foot to slow his momentum until he came to a stop ten feet from Amanda.

If she was shocked to see him, she didn't show it. In fact, when her eyes snapped open, she scowled up at him seemingly annoyed at his sudden arrival.

Shifting from her knees to drop onto her ass, she kicked at the axe near her before glaring up at him. "What do you want?"

Honestly, he didn't know how to answer that. He needed to apologize, but what he really *wanted* was to go back to last night. He wanted to force himself to be in the moment instead of staring into the fire, lost in thoughts. He wanted to pay attention to the stories and chatter all around him. He wanted to realize when things were winding down so that when Amanda placed a hand on his knee to help herself up, he wouldn't have reacted. She'd caught him off guard, and he'd acted on instinct, and none of that was her fault. No, it was one hundred percent on him. He was a stage five Skin Walker for Christ's sake. He should have exhibited better control. He should have been paying attention. He should have been present. But how did he express that to the raven-haired beauty glaring up at him mutinously from the ground. He couldn't, so wordlessly, he bent and snatched up the axe.

Without saying anything, he stacked the toppled log, and with one smooth movement, he swung the axe effortlessly over his head and drove it through the log. It split easily. Grabbing another log, he ignored Amanda's soft snort. In his periphery he saw her roll her eyes before she got to her feet and stomped toward the front of the cabin still cradling her arm. He didn't expect a thank you, but he didn't expect to be ignored either. As he continued to chop her wood, he wondered if this was how Remy felt. Maybe Amanda was the reason their relationship hadn't been working out.

Mason chopped until the entire cord of wood stacked against the house was split and re-stacked into even piles. He wasn't even sweating from the exertion as he leaned the handle of the axe against his thigh and propped his hands on his hips, admiring his stack of cut wood. It should be enough to last Amanda a few weeks, but it was supposed to get cold soon. Cold up here meant several feet of snow and blistering temps that dipped well below zero.

Lifting a hand to scratch at the back of his head, Mason wondered how difficult it'd be to run a gas line from StoneCrow Estates to Amanda's cabin. As CFO for StoneCrow, he knew that Monroe had paid an obscene amount of money for the amenity on his vast Estate. Glancing at Amanda's cabin, Mason knew it was an expense she couldn't afford, so he made a mental note to have several more cords of wood delivered and to look into a propane tank at the very least.

Dusting splinters and chunks of wood off his sweater and jeans as he circled the cabin, he cleaned himself up as best he could before stopping at the bottom of the stairs leading up to the front door. He needed to apologize to Amanda, but was having difficulty bringing himself to do it. She'd want to know why he acted the way he had, and she deserved to know, but he was reluctant about explaining.

Just six short years ago, Mason had discovered the identity of his birth father. One of Monroe's teams had raided a facility housing captured Skin Walkers. The computers, files, and samples seized had helped Monroe begin his database registry on Skin Walkers. It's how they'd made a match to Mason's DNA. One of the captives, a male named Huron was Mason's father. A father he didn't remember. A father he'd never know. A father who'd been forced into a breeding program. From the recorded date of his father's capture, Mason knew that he was born prior to his father's capture; but that's all they knew about Mason's story. There was no information on Mason's birth or his birth mother, just a match to Huron. Raised by adopted parents who'd acquired him from an orphanage in England, there'd been no trail for Mason to follow. It had almost been like he'd manifested from nothing, just simply arrived at the orphanage, no history, no records. And in the records they'd seized from the Megalya facility, there'd been no mention of a mate for Huron, only a note that while in captivity, he'd been forced into a breeding program where he'd successfully impregnated a human female. The resulting child, a little girl, was taken from the facility after it was discovered that she held none of Huron's Walker abilities. One lone note, a mere word gave Mason hope that she was still alive. Abandoned. It was the lone word stamped across the notes on his sister's birth record. Other notations showed that her human mother had died during delivery. Mason had been on the hunt for his younger sibling since they'd made the discovery of her existence.

Sighing at the painful memories, Mason snorted.

A child?

His sister would be twenty-seven now. Ten years younger than him, sure, but by no means a child.

Turning away from the cabin, Mason stalked toward the woods. He couldn't apologize to Amanda. He didn't want to talk right now, not to anyone. The pain squeezing his heart was making it difficult to breathe, so he stalked back toward StoneCrow, resolved to show Amanda with actions—rather than words—how sorry he was. He'd make things right because Amanda was a good friend to the Walkers at StoneCrow. She deserved better than to be hurt by any of them, especially by a male who couldn't get his mind off his own regrets. The possibility that his sister was dead was very real, and the longer the search went on, the more years that passed, the more Mason found himself considering that possibility. He hated the thought of failing his sister and his father. He wanted her back, he wanted his family whole, but each passing year that seemed less and less likely.

Still, none of that had a thing to do with Amanda Chandler. She was innocent, and unaware of just how fucked up Mason was. If she had even the slightest clue just how out of it he was all the time, she'd have never claimed a seat beside him at the bonfire.

She'd have kept her damn distance. With any luck, she'd realize it now and steer clear of him from here on out.

Chapter 5

Amanda woke sore. She'd really fucked her arm up trying to chop wood yesterday, and while it made her even more mad at Mason, she stalled in bed wondering why he'd come to her cabin yesterday. Obviously, he'd chopped her wood out of guilt, but he hadn't apologized and that bothered her. When people did something wrong, they were supposed to apologize. Remy had never apologized for getting her attached to him and then ditching her like she was just some casual play thing. And now, Mason's lack of apology for hurting her had her wondering if these Skin Walkers were incapable of admitting when they were wrong.

Rolling to her side, she used a hand to pull her star quilt tighter around her bad shoulder. Glancing at the clock, she heaved a weary sigh knowing today was going to be just as long and arduous as yesterday. Hell, just getting showered and dressed was going to be a monumental effort.

In the kitchen, the sound of the coffee maker clicking on was followed by pops and clicks before she heard the tell-tale drips of the dark nectar slowly filling the pot. Amanda didn't have a lot of money, but she'd splurged last Christmas and bought Remy one of those new programmable coffee makers. When he hadn't shown up on Christmas Eve or Christmas day, she'd unwrapped the gift and decided to keep it for herself, and she hadn't regretted one second of her decision.

Staring at the wall as her cabin slowly filled with the mouth-watering aroma of her favored vanilla flavored dark roast, Amanda seriously considered just staying in bed all day. It couldn't happen, but God, it was nice to wish.

Heaving another weighty sigh, she reluctantly tossed the blankets off and cringed when her bare feet touched the cold wooden planks of the floor. Last night, she'd been too stubborn to go out and collect some of the wood Mason had chopped, which meant that when her fire had burned out at around four this morning, she'd just had to suffer from her foolish choice. Damned foolish pride.

An hour and a half after Amanda had started getting ready for the day, she was finally finished. Showering and washing her hair were all extremely difficult to do with one arm. Brushing her hair hadn't been any easier, and pulling a pair of worn skinny jeans over a pair of equally tight thermal bottoms had been nearly impossible. Donning her socks and hiking boots had her sprawled out on her bed like a giant starfish as she panted, sweat dotting her forehead and nose from her efforts. She was fully dressed from the waist down and heaved heavy breaths as she lay sprawled in a satin bra that had taken a gargantuan effort to get into. She'd saved her sweater for last, knowing it'd be the hardest thing to get into. It didn't disappoint. Bending her bad arm to get into the sleeve was excruciating and had her thinking she'd just sleep in the sweater tonight or cut it off to get out of it. Winded, Amanda cursed herself for not having just stayed in bed. Glancing at the clock, she cursed and rushed from her bedroom. Grabbing her keys off the peg near the door, she hit auto start and paused to listen for the motor to come to life. It did. *Barely*. Fishing her cell out of her back pocket, she pulled up Google. The other night when she'd gone to the E.R., her truck had barely made it back to the Highwoods. Because it was her sole means of transportation, she needed to get it fixed and she needed it done ASAP because according to the news, snow—the real stuff, not the near foot she'd been enduring—was on its way soon.

Scrolling through Google's top auto repair shops, she sought out one that claimed to be fast and cheap before she hit the call button for a place with the four stars but two dollar signs. Acceptable work at a cheap price. Just what she needed.

Ten minutes later, purse in tow, she was in her truck, bumping down the mountain with her bad arm in its sling and held tight against her body. In her head, she was doing the math trying to figure out how she was supposed to pay for her E.R. visit and the repairs her truck would need. She had twelve hundred dollars in savings, and was hoping the doctor's visit would only be around six hundred even with the X-rays they took. That would leave her six hundred dollars for truck repairs.

For four years, Amanda had been an administrative assistant for a local financial services holding company. They'd laid her off last year, right about the time Remy had slowed his frequent visits. It had made for a wretched holiday season, but the new year brought new hope. A small school in the tiniest of rural towns, less than a hundred miles east of her cabin had hired her on as a math teacher. It was great. She liked numbers and liked the kids even more; the only problem was that the pay was shit. Luckily, her cabin was paid off or she'd never have been able to survive. Still, things were tight and she went without a lot simply because she couldn't afford frivolities. She was proud though that she'd built up some money in savings for times such as these.

Emergencies! That's what this was, so there was little guilt in knowing she'd probably be snuffing out her reserves and have to start all over again after the next few weeks were through.

Trying to find the silver lining, she concentrated on the fact that while her savings would be empty, she wouldn't be deeper in debt. She couldn't afford to dig herself any deeper. She was maxed out.

An hour and forty minutes later Amanda was standing, teary-eyed, begging with the auto shop owner.

Oh God, no! No, no, no, no, no! "Please," Amanda cried, "I don't have sixteen hundred dollars!" She held up the fist-full of dollars in her hand that she'd just withdrawn from her bank. "Six hundred! That's what you originally quoted me, thirty minutes

ago! Six hundred dollars! It's all I have!"

"Yeah," the jerk in greased up coveralls behind the counter

drawled as he chewed on the stub of a snuffed out cigar that

Amanda could smell even across the counter. "The three hundred

was for the tow and the new battery."

"Three hundred dollars for a tow and a battery?" she

shrieked incredulously. "How much is a battery?" She didn't let

him respond before she rushed on. "The tow couldn't be that

much!" She jerked her thumb over her shoulder pleading, "I broke

down a block away. Literally *one block* away!"

The guy continued without an ounce of remorse, "But it

needs a lot more work. We gotta do more diagnostic tests, and

there'll be parts to pay for. Plus, there's the seventy-five dollars a

day in labor, which is pretty darn cheap considering I *could* charge

you more." He chomped some more on his cigar. "Thirteen-

hundred more dollars."

"Seventy-five dollar a day labor?" Amanda huffed in

disbelief looking down at the desk and slowly shaking her head.

"That…that's not even right." Her head shot up and she narrowed her eyes on the guy. "You don't know how long it's gonna take to fix my truck. What if it's only a day? That's only seventy five dollars! You're trying to pre-charge me for labor you haven't even done yet!"

The guy's cheek ticked up and he shrugged with zero emotion, "Processing fees."

"Please," Amanda begged holding up her cash. "You said six hundred. I can…I can get the rest," she finally admitted reluctantly knowing she'd be screwed on her medical bills and would have to borrow a little from Lilly or Cindy. "I'll just need time to get it. I'm waiting to get paid," she lied hoping to buy time. "Is that okay." She slapped her money on the counter and shoved it toward him. "Okay?"

"Look…." The guy stared Amanda up and down, brows spearing down as his lip curled up. "Lady, you want your truck fixed, you pay the cost."

He was getting angry now and Amanda knew it wasn't going to help her case.

Blowing out a slow breath, she tried to calm herself as she started again, "Look…" Her eye dipped to the patch sewn just above his right pocket. "*Earl*. We're both working people. You've gotta understand how tight money can be." Gingerly, she shrugged up her slinged arm and rested it on the counter before lifting her purse, taking out her wallet and making a show of opening it in front of him. Pulling out the stack of twenties inside, she felt her stomach tighten with dread at the prospect of spending this month's bill money. She knew it was exactly one hundred dollars and the measly forty dollars she'd have left over after dropping sixty on food was supposed to be for gas and even that would barely get her to and from work.

"I can," she flipped through the money, counting it in front of him even though she knew exactly how much was there. "I can give you everything I've got." She pulled out a single twenty and stuffed it in her bra. "Except twenty, which I need for gas. I have to get to and from work."

Earl's eyes slid from where she'd tucked the money into her bra to the cash in her hand, and Amanda felt a little surge of hope.

"Eighty more dollars." She slapped the eighty on top of the pile with the rest of her money. "Six hundred and eighty total. Please," she begged. "It's all I've got right now." She gave him her most pathetic look because at this point, she wasn't above begging.

Driving to this shop, Amanda's truck had choked to a halt a measly block away. Grateful she was so close, Amanda had called this shop and when Earl had shown up, she thought he was a knight in greasy armor. That dream died a quick death. The old jerk didn't even talk to or look at her as he anchored up her truck and lifted the front end with his. They'd ridden the single block in silence, Amanda sitting shotgun beside him and trying to make friendly talk, which he ignored. Once they got to the shop, he told her to wait in a dirty chair next to a desk out front while he assessed the situation. Without asking or even telling her, he'd changed out the battery and then run some more tests.

When she'd driven it to town, she'd been confident that her truck just needed an oil change or spark plugs or something equally as cheap. It had been wishful thinking on her part because she knew it was all she could afford. If she'd only had to worry about her recent E.R. visit, her student loans, truck insurance, utilities, and groceries, Amanda might have had a little breathing room, but last year she'd gotten sick. She'd been so ill that she'd passed out at work and they'd called an ambulance to take her to the hospital, where she spent three days with pneumonia, an ear infection, and a concussion from where her head had cracked off her desk when she'd passed out. She'd even suspected her passing out in the office was the reason she'd been fired from her administrative assistant position. They didn't want the liability. So, here she sat. One ambulance ride, three days in the hospital, and twelve thousand, two hundred and sixty-six dollars in debt later, she was drowning, and no one cared. No one was throwing out a life-line and that's not how things were supposed to work. When you were a good person and you went to work every day to pay your bills, things were supposed to work in your favor. Right?

That's what all the TV shows and books said. It's what all those lying-ass fairy tales she'd read as a little girl let her believe. But life wasn't a fairytale. Far fucking from it, and right now, good person or not, the world didn't give a damn about the debt trying it's damnedest to swallow her up whole. She hated being forced to beg, to humble herself to kiss the ass of someone so callous and rude. What had started out feeling like being stuck in mud now felt like being trapped in quicksand. Amanda was sinking deeper and deeper and the more she struggled against it, the worse it got.

"Please," she quaked again, sucking back stinging tears of humiliation and rage.

Earl looked at her cash, looked at her, then back to the money. "You owe sixteen, sweet cheeks. Six hundred and eighty ain't gonna cut it."

"What about holding it for me out in the yard until I can get you the money?" She glanced at the clock. Just her damn luck that the bank had just closed. She could get his money, but it'd have to wait until tomorrow, which meant she'd need to bum a ride back home and then back to town tomorrow or she'd have to spend some of her precious cash on a cheap room for the night.

Pulling his cigar free from his lips, he shook his head and replied with a gruff, "Hundred dollars a day holding fee."

That was it. She didn't have enough money, and he wasn't going to budge. There was no other argument to be made. There was no other way.

Defeat pressed heavily on her chest leaving her feeling gutted…hollow. Sniffing and curling her fist around the cash on the counter, Amanda lowered her head and nodded. She didn't want this jerk to see the defeat she knew was etched onto her face. He didn't deserve to see it even if she *was* defeated. Walking out of here now without her truck meant leaving it behind for good.

The old Dodge Ram had cost her fifteen hundred dollars when she'd bought it four years ago even though the front fender was primer gray and didn't match the rest of the truck's hunter green paint. Still, even though it was old and not particularly attractive, it was in decent shape, and she'd taken good care of it. She'd named it Hunter because of the color, and she'd taken care of it as best she could. It had been her dad's, and after he'd died and left her the cabin, she'd hunted down the truck too. The cabin and the truck needed to go together. It felt like she had more a connection with her dad to have both back together again. She hadn't missed an oil change, she bought new tires one at a time until she had a full set. She'd even splurged one payday before the hospital bills had started pouring in and bought all new seat covers and floor mats. But, there was no way she could justify spending more to get it home than she'd spent to actually buy it, especially when that money wasn't for upgrades or any form of maintenance. If it was three hundred dollars to tow it a block and throw a battery in it then there was no way she could even pay to have to towed back home, and the hundred dollar a day holding fee—even though it was bullshit—was still a sum she couldn't afford.

Snatching her money off the counter, Amanda crammed it into her purse with one hand as she felt the sting of humiliation creep up her neck and land heavily in her cheeks.

She hated this so goddamn much! She hated this feeling with the strength of a thousand suns. She felt degraded and embarrassed and…poor.

"Thank you for everything," she muttered without looking up at Earl. The guy was a first-class asshole, but she wasn't going to dignify his shitty behavior with the outburst that he rightly deserved.

Turning, she startled when she collided with a solid chest. Strong arms shot out and caught her gently just as she was stumbling backward. Head snapping up, she saw Mason glaring over her head at Earl.

Chapter 6

Shocked into silence by Mason's sudden appearance, Amanda simply blinked up at him.

His pecan-colored hair was combed back in a style that looked like he'd just stepped off the pages of GQ. Wearing a gray herringbone tweed suit that would look ridiculous on anyone else, it was tailored to his stunning physique. His shoulders were broad and powerful beneath the crisp white collar of his shirt and black satin tie overtop. Amanda watched a vein throb in a neck that was thick with muscle.

Trying to mask the shiver of whatever it was that coursed through her, Amanda jerked back to reality as shame washed over her anew. Pulling her hands from where they had settled on Mason's chest, she stepped back. Had Mason witnessed her humiliation? Things like this probably never happened to him. This type of treatment was probably so foreign to a man like him that he probably didn't know whether to laugh or simply keep enjoying the show.

"You can't do that," Mason boomed in his thick English accent.

Holy hell!

That accent coupled with his anger on her behalf unfurled something molten low in Amanda's belly. It was something she struggled to ignore as she tried to back up further.

Undeterred, Mason kept his hold firmly on her good arm, releasing her injured one as he raged, "You can't charge her for labor you haven't done!"

"It's fine," Amanda muttered, but Mason ignored her.

"I-it's on the books," Earl stammered behind her. "It's *gonna* get done."

Mason thundered, "But it's not now, is it?"

Staring up at him, Amanda was dazed by how he was coming to her defense. Whether it was because he felt guilty about her arm or for some other reason, she didn't know. She was grateful all the same because Earl was hemming and hawing now, and she felt just a tinge of gratification that the tables had turned.

"You're going to fix her truck," Mason commanded. "Then you're going to mail out an itemized bill, and if there are any fraudulent charges for parts *or* labor, we'll take it up with the court."

Finally gathering himself, Earl cleared his throat and growled, "And what if I just put her piece of shit truck out on the street; or better yet, I could have it impounded for non-payment."

Eyes flashing dangerously now, Mason snarled, "Fucking try it."

Staring up at Mason, Amanda blinked. Her mouth fell open when his pupils blew out and obliterated all color, going fully matte black.

Shit, shit, shit! Quickly glancing around the front office, Amanda wondered what would happen if Mason shifted here.

Placing a hand on his chest to calm him, she gave him a little shove, almost afraid to do even that. "It's alright," she began quietly. "Just forget about it."

Mason's dark eyes shot down to hers. "No!" His eyes slid back up to Earl. "This behavior is unacceptable." But this time when he spoke, his voice was eerily low and calm.

Goose bumps blasted up Amanda's arms and she knew that if *she* was afraid then Earl was probably shitting himself. Granted, he had no idea why Mason's eyes were blacked out or why his incisors were slowly elongating.

"Mason," Amanda breathed, stepping more fully into him so he could hear her, she quietly hissed, "Don't do this here!"

Nostrils flaring, chest heaving, Mason's angry eyes dipped to hers again and this time they held.

Having his full attention on her stole Amanda's breath. Yeah, he'd hurt her at the bonfire, but he'd been distracted then, he hadn't been focusing on her. And when he came to her cabin following the incident, he still hadn't done more than cast her a cursory glance. Now, though, his blacked out eyes stayed locked on her. It was unnerving and a little exhilarating. Still, she couldn't let him shift in the jerk's shop even as much as the ass deserved the shock of a lifetime or to be mauled by whatever form Mason took.

"Please," she pleaded quietly. "Don't expose yourself over me. I'm not worth it."

His eyes thinned to narrowed slits. When he finally spoke, his gravelly voice sent chills blasting up her spine. "Who the fuck let you believe that? Remy?" He jerked his chin toward the guy behind the counter. "This fuck?" He took a step toward Earl, and Amanda had to shift her body to keep herself between Mason and the desk.

Oh God, am I just making things worse.

"No," she rushed out, flattening a hand on his chest. "No one let me believe it. I just…" Just what? Had shit self-esteem? Shaking her head, she frowned up at Mason. "Just leave it. It's not your problem. *I'm* not your problem. Besides, it's just a vehicle. I'll figure it out."

"No," he fumed, angry eyes going back to Earl. "I'll figure it out. Go wait in the car."

Go wait in the car? Indignation flared at the order. First, he'd manhandled her, then he'd failed to apologize, and now he was ordering her around. Who in the hell did Mason EnemyHunter think he was?

Turning, Amanda glared at Earl. "I've got to make a few calls. Don't do anything with my truck yet. I'll be in touch soon." Shoulder checking Mason as best she could as she passed Amanda had to grit her teeth at the wave of pain the foolish action caused. She knew better than that. Trying to move a Walker was like trying to move a damn mountain, and Mason was no exception. The man's shoulders were as broad as a barn and he towered at least a foot and half above her. He was fast too. So fast that Amanda didn't make it more than a step before his hand shot out and gripped her good wrist. Unable to leave, she whipped her head around to glare up at him mutinously with a gritted out, "Don't!"

Chapter 7

Mason's intention when he'd followed Amanda to town late that afternoon was to be a passive observer. She piqued his curiosity in a way no one had in a long time. Perhaps it was because he had his head so focused on the past that he hadn't really noticed much about the world that had been passing him by. He'd been preoccupied to the point of distraction, up until he'd wrenched Amanda's arm at the bonfire. Now, towering over her, having her tiny wrist clamped in his hand, strange emotions began to bubble to the surface.

Looking down into her angry eyes, he could scent her humiliation. It pissed him off that any man would intentionally try to shame a woman, and when Amanda had uttered, "I'm not worth it," Mason wanted to rage at the scent of untainted truth that filled the air. She honestly believed she wasn't worth a fight.

Fucking piece of shit, Remy McCabe!

How dare he keep a human and not make her feel significant. How dare he fail to covet what he had.

It wasn't unheard of in Skin Walker society for their kind to hook up with females who weren't their Angels. Hell, most of them would never find their one true mate, and expecting grown males, fully in their prime, to remain celibate because of it was ridiculous. Lots of flings or short relationships occurred, but Mason had never once heard of a male Skin Walker treating a female as shamefully as Remy had been treating Amanda. Remy had several "girlfriends" at any given moment. Most other Walkers weren't bothered by it because Remy hadn't ever really committed to any of the women. At least, that's what they'd all thought, but the more Mason had looked into Remy's relationship with Amanda, the more he realized that Remy had let her believe that their relationship was serious and exclusive when it wasn't. Amanda had invested her heart into their relationship and Remy hadn't done the same. It was sickening. Remy's actions made Amanda look foolish and judging by the humiliation pouring from her now over something so simple as a vehicle, Mason knew she'd be more than devastated if she knew the truth about Remy. She'd be hurt and embarrassed. Remy was disgracing this poor woman and she didn't even know it. He wanted to blame Amanda. She should have known better. Shouldn't she? *Aww, hell!* How did he get so deep into this already?

The prick behind the counter drew Mason's attention when he growled an angry, "Hey!"

It had Mason's brows spearing down even deeper as his lip ticked up. He flashed the guy a snarl that had him instantly falling silent. Eyes going back to Amanda, Mason said, "Go wait in my car." Tacking on a forced, "Please," he waited for her to do his bidding. But Amanda didn't move, so he let his animals pollute his voice when he raged, "Get in the bloody car, Amanda!"

She glanced in uncertainty between him and the crook behind the counter before she offered a little huff of resignation, pulled her wrist free of his grasp, and walked out. The bell over the door chimed behind her and finally alone with the asshole, Mason let him have it.

Short minutes later, Mason strode out of the shop. Confident that Amanda's vehicle would receive the best service, he'd also ensured that he'd be billed because he'd overheard nearly the entire conversation earlier and knew Amanda couldn't afford the required services.

Stepping onto the sidewalk, his eyes locked with Amanda's where she sat in the passenger seat of the only car in the parking lot, his gunmetal gray Dodger Challenger. For a heartbeat, he couldn't help but think how good she looked sitting shotgun. Then another realization struck. He'd never had a woman in his car before. Ever.

Dismissing the thought, he strode to the driver's side, his eyes still drinking in the sight of Amanda, disregarding his internal demand to focus on anything but her. Her hair was so black that it winked with near purple highlights. Her eyes were dark brown, and she had a scar that bisected her delicate right eyebrow. He was curious as hell about how she got it, but knew he'd never ask.

Beautiful. Too *beautiful for the likes of Remy McCabe.*

Sliding into the driver's seat, he sat in silence a moment, wondering if anything needed to be said before he ushered her back to the Highwood Mountains. Deciding they'd said all that needed saying, he started his car, the familiar throaty purr of the engine making him feel almost guilty.

"Nice car," Amanda mumbled.

The comment had him feeling the need to make an excuse for such extravagance. "It's the only thing I've ever splurged on."

"You didn't apologize," she accused quietly.

Her abrupt change of conversation threw him for a moment. He swallowed thickly knowing exactly what she was talking about.

When he didn't speak, she continued, "When someone hurts you for no reason, they're supposed to apologize."

Turning his head, he stared at her while she kept her face stoically forward. The slight scent of humiliation still lingered, but now it was accompanied by the spicy flare of anger, which he preferred. Her anger gave him something to work with because it didn't have his inner beasts snarling and clawing at his insides to defend her. Looking at her, he let sincerity fill his voice as his eyes dipped to where her arm rested in its sling. "I am sorry, Amanda."

She blinked and then there were tears in her eyes which only served to make his apology feel insufficient.

"I shouldn't have touched you in anger," he continued. Looking forward, he fisted the steering wheel and heaved a weighty sigh. "I shouldn't have touched you *at all*. But I'll pay the medical bills."

"Paying my bills doesn't take it away," she snapped, and when he didn't respond she said, "And neither does chopping my fire wood."

"I know," he admitted quietly, not sure why he hadn't already apologized and gotten it over with. "I should have said the words that day, but…"

"But what?"

Without answering, he backed his car out of the parking lot and turned it onto main street. Great Falls was a small town, but not so small that they couldn't have taken Amanda's car to another shop. It was the principle though that had Mason shooting the dingy engine repair shop a dirty look in the rearview mirror.

Amanda let him drive them a few blocks before she demanded again, "But what, Mason?"

"I don't know." He fisted the steering wheel and glanced out his side window trying to get his bearings. This woman threw him off kilter and no one had done that in a very long time. After stalling a moment, he finally admitted, "I didn't know how to apologize for what I'd done because I'm still not certain what came over me. You touched me and I lost it. I just... I was..."

"Preoccupied," she supplied, staring straight ahead.

He glanced at her and then put his eyes back on the road. The tension in the car was stifling and he couldn't figure out if it was because of her or because of his reaction to her.

"Yeah," he clipped out.

"I've seen you around the estate a lot. Your head's always in the clouds."

Her admission shocked him because while he knew who she was, he didn't remember seeing her "a lot." So, unsure how to respond, he didn't.

"Maybe if you interacted more, you wouldn't be so averse to humans."

His head whipped around and his eyes narrowed on her. "Is that what you think happened? You think I don't like humans?"

She shrugged and the motion lifted her arm in its sling, drawing his eyes to it.

"I don't dislike humans, Amanda."

Turning her head, she stared out her window and muttered, "Just me then."

"It wasn't you either. I was caught off guard. I was…" Unable to find a better word he cursed and heaved a repeated and distinctly insufficient, "preoccupied."

"With what?" she demanded. "Can you at least tell me that."

But he couldn't. Only a few select people knew about his search for his sister and that's the way he wanted to keep it. He didn't want or need people feeling sorry for him, and he sure as shit didn't want people offering him advice or their suggestions on all he *should* be doing. But mostly he didn't want people knowing about his search for his sister because he didn't want them constantly asking how the search was going. It'd be a constant reminder that he was failing. Monroe was willing to send out teams to follow-up on Mason's leads, but all of those leads had turned up nothing. And with each disappointment, Mason was forced to consider the possibility that his sister might be dead. Accepting it was nearly impossible and having to face the prospect of never finding her brought on crushing anxiety. So, he lied. "It's difficult work doing all the accounting for an Estate the size of StoneCrow." "It's a stressful job and Mr. StoneCrow's penchant for spending is off the charts, making my job much more difficult."

When she glanced at him, he felt the full weight of her scrutiny. She was sizing him up.

Before she could interrogate him, he quickly changed the subject. "Why don't you have enough money to get your car fixed. Surely, you have savings." The words came out way more accusatory than he'd intended.

Amanda's expression changed in an instant and the look she shot him had him barely hiding a wince.

"Why were you at the repair shop?" she snarked back.

Shhhhhit!

Mind racing for an excuse he blurted out, "Well, my car..." His words tapered off when he realized he couldn't lie about it needing attention because they were currently gliding smoothly down the road inside of it. So instead of lying to Amanda, he guided his car off the road and into the parking lot of a restaurant that he knew served excellent steak and had great selection of wine.

Amanda's attention left him when the car stopped. Leaning forward, she eyed the storefront. "What's this?"

"Dinner. I'm hungry. You?" He didn't wait for her to answer before he was climbing out of the car then hurrying around to open her door. Pulling it open he offered her a hand, but she simply stared up at him.

Suspicion laced her tone when she asked, "What are you doing?"

"Eating before I head home. Since you need a ride, you're forced to accompany me." He glanced at the restaurant then back at her and shook his proffered hand. "Come on, the food here is fabulous. I promise."

Amanda didn't budge. "Tell me what you were doing at the shop, Mason. Were you following me?"

He absolutely was, and he absolutely wasn't about to admit it.

"I just happened to be in town and needed to run by the shop." *Christ!* The excuse sounded lame even to his own ears.

Crossing her good arm under her slinged arm, Amanda groused, "If you're going to keep lying to me, I'm just gonna walk home."

She made to get out of the car, but Mason planted his big body in her way, cutting off her escape.

"*Keep* lying? I haven't lied to you once," he lied for the dozenth time.

"You said you're always preoccupied because your job is stressful, but I've seen your face, Mason. When you're staring at your phone or looking into that locket you carry."

Her words rocked him because he only ever looked at the locket when he was certain he was alone. Knowing he'd been caught staring at it, that Amanda had seen him at his most vulnerable, was jarring.

Amanda continued, "The emotion on your face when you're looking at those things isn't stress from difficult math or frustration from Monroe's overspending." Turning her head, she stared at the restaurant. "It's the same look you had at the bonfire. You're not overwhelmed or *preoccupied*. You're...*sad*."

How? How did this woman know so much about him when he knew so little about her? And why did he know so little about her? She was intriguing, and distracting, and...still sitting in the car leaving him with a hand still out waiting on her and looking like a fool.

Dropping his hand, he sighed and stared over the car. Propping one arm on the opened door and the other on the roof of the vehicle, he drew in a deep breath of arctic air that stung his nostril and burned his lungs. It felt good. Exhaling the breath on a pent-up breath that left his lips on a frigid cloud, he muttered flatly, "Amanda, I'm trying here." He dropped his eyes to her. "I don't hurt women. *Ever!* And I hurt you. I can't explain it, and I know that doesn't make it alright, but I'm trying to make it up to you the only way I know how." Lifting a hand, he buried it in his hair and fisted the satiny strands. "I'm gonna chop your firewood and I'm gonna pay your medical bills."

She frowned up at him and opened her mouth to protest, but he held up a hand.

"And I'm going to make sure your truck is fixed up right and I'm paying for that too. But now," he dropped his arms and dropped down into a squat in front of her that brought him eye level because of his impressive height. *"Right now,* I just need to feed you. I'm asking you to give me that. I know I don't deserve for you to give me anything, but I'm asking all the same."

A moment of guilt flashed across her soft features before she was able to mask it and Mason knew he had her. Inwardly, he grinned inwardly at her soft heart.

"Fine," she bit out and stood, crowding him so that he was forced to shoot to his feet and back up to give her space. "I'll pay for my own truck repairs, but dinner would be nice," she admitted. "I'm hungry."

Something about her admission of hunger had his hands clenching into fists. His inner beasts didn't like knowing she was needing in their presence, and it drew up fierce protective instincts. It was the second time that'd happened in just an hour. Swallowing hard, Mason shoved the inappropriate instincts back where they belonged. He had no damn business feeling *anything* where Amanda was concerned, and the last thing he needed was his animals feeling any type of responsibility for her. She had Remy, and all Mason needed to do was help with her bills, truck—regardless of what she said--, and chores at her cabin until she was healed then his guilt would be assuaged. He was sure of it.

Reaching down to grab Amanda's hand, his body jerked when a jolt of pain shot through him from where their skin made contact. Amanda felt it too because she gasped and jerked her hand back before glaring down at it. Turning it over she looked at the back of her hand and then at her palm before she breathed, "What the hell was that?"

Mason was frowning down at his hand too. "Static electricity." Balling his hand into a fist and then un-balling it, he stepped back and motioned for Amanda to precede him.

She skirted past him like she was afraid that further contact would incite another shock. Backing up, Mason gave Amanda a wide berth as he glanced down at his hand again. That hadn't been static electricity. It had been something else entirely. But what?

Chapter 8

Inside the restaurant, Mason spoke with the hostess then nearly settled a hand on Amanda's lower back to steer her to follow the hostess before he quickly jerked his hand back. Extending an arm instead, he ushered Amanda ahead of him as he followed behind without touching her.

At the table, he pulled out Amanda's chair and stalled. Instinct dictated he offer to help her remove her coat, but just now realizing she wasn't wearing one, he had to tamp down a spike of disapproval. "No coat?" he bit out, not bothering to hide the censure in his tone.

Glancing down at herself and then up at him, Amanda frowned. "It took me over an hour just to get *these* clothes on. Figured I'd forego a coat."

"And if your truck had broken down?"

She shot him a look then quickly flipped opened her menu, but the tell-tale color flooding her cheeks had his temper flaring.

"You broke down? Without a coat?"

"Shhhh," Amanda hissed, glancing between the tables on either side of them. "It was only a few blocks."

"A few blocks? And what if it had happened in the mountains? Or on the highway?"

She huffed a delicate sound. "I'd have managed."

"You know," he gritted out, leaning across the table as his eyes held hers intently. "For someone who's supposed to be a hardened mountain woman, you make some real shit decisions."

Slapping the menu closed, Amanda leaned across the table too. "My decisions are none of your business. Neither is my coat or my truck or my firewood." Shoving her chair back, she made to stand, but Mason clamped a firm hand over her much smaller one that rested atop the menu. Another jolt tore through him, but this time he held firm. Letting the strange energy pass from Amanda to him even when she inhaled sharply and glanced down at their hands.

"Wait." He drew her attention with his command and when Amanda's eyes slid up to meet his, her brows furrowed in a dainty glare.

Rising to his feet, Mason kept his hand over hers. Dipping his chin placatingly, he said, "I apologize. That was rude. *I* was rude. Please." He motioned toward her menu with his free hand. "Stay."

Swallowing hard, Amanda blinked up at him before slowly relaxing into her seat and scooting it closer to the table.

Mason released her hand and sighed quietly, relieved he'd diffused the situation. Taking up his own menu, he pretended to look it over. Instead, his gaze slid up the page and landed on the woman seated across from him. While Amanda concentrated on her menu, Mason tried not to stare at her but the intensity with which she studied it gave him the opportunity to finally take her in. She was attractive as hell and being lame with her arm in its sling once again had his protective instincts surging to the fore. Maybe it was the way that fuck at the garage had treated her or maybe it was the way her slender fingers held the edge of the menu almost delicately, whatever it was, *something* about her had Mason thinking she was too damn fragile in her current state to be out dealing with assholes like garage fuck. Silently, he regarded her, taking in her soft features. It wasn't until her brows furrowed that he realized he was staring.

Clearing his throat and glancing down at his own menu, he asked casually before looking back up, "Something wrong?"

Still frowning at the menu, Amanda looked perplexed. Her eyes sliced to his then back down. "I know you're supposed to have red wine with red meat, but..."

"But what?"

She looked up and her cheeks heated with an attractive blush as she whispered conspiratorially, "I like white wine."

A burst of some foreign emotion zinged through his insides like a fiery little shooting star. It had him reclining back in his seat to admire her. And admire he did, but didn't truly understand it. What was it about her? Something about her, about her whispered little admission had him beaming with approval.

"Get what you want, Amanda. Don't let societal conventions dictate what *you're* having for dinner. It's nobody's damn business what you like. It's yours."

Lifting a hand, he gestured to the waiter who rushed over. Not wanting Amanda to be put on the spot, Mason said, "I'll have the house pinot grigio." He slid his gaze to her as a pleased grin lit up her face. Eyes sparkling, she looked from Mason to the waiter with a relieved, "Me too!"

It was official, Monroe was right. He needed to get out more. He needed socializing because gifting something so simple as a glass of white wine with no judgement to Amanda had him feeling like a goddamn God. And that had him worried. This shit needed to stop and it needed to stop *now*!

What in the bloody hell am I doing?

Forcing himself to keep his eyes off Amanda as their wine was delivered, he took a quick sip, snubbing her proffered glass for a toast and pretended not to see it as he intently studied the menu not really seeing it.

With a feminine snort, Amanda shrugged up one shoulder and then took a sip of her wine which was followed with a moan of approval as her eyes drifted closed.

The sound she emitted had Mason's eyes narrowing on her mouth. Something low in his belly tightened and he had to swallow hard to force some strange emotion back down. When Amanda's eyes blinked open, her amber gaze landed on Mason and he liked it. He liked being the focus of her attention. And that shit wasn't going to work.

Clearing his throat abruptly, he tore his attention from Amanda and motioned for the waiter, determined to get through dinner and to get Amanda back home ASAP. He hadn't spent this much time with a single person in…well, for a very long time, and it was throwing him off kilter, and *that* he didn't like. Mason prided himself on his absolute control in all situations. It's why his attack on Amanda had thrown him so hard, and now here he was trying to make amends and letting his control slip again. It couldn't happen. It wouldn't!

In short order, they ordered their dinner and then it was just the two of them, sitting in an uncomfortable silence as Mason looked everywhere but at the woman seated across from him. Typically, he'd eat dinner in his suite at the Manor while he poured over intel and leads on his sister. Honestly, this was the first time in as long as he could remember that he actually took a meal and paid any attention to it. It was different, it was...nice, even if he was being rude and ignoring Amanda. They ate in a companionable silence, aside from her comments on how good the steaks and loaded baked potatoes were. When the waiter asked, Amanda refused dessert and Mason did the same, opting for a coffee instead. Their plates were taken after the meal and with nothing else to concentrate on, he had no choice but to give his attention back to Amanda as he waited for his coffee.

Chin resting in her upraised palm, Amanda stared absently out the window while Mason's coffee was settled in front of him. It was getting dark fast. It always did in Montana winters, and as the sun gave up its light to the bitterly cold dark, Mason reclined in his seat, taking slow sips of his coffee as he watched Amanda just as closely as she was watching the world beyond the window. With her face angled away from him, he could make out details he hadn't noticed before. The scar through her eyebrow was more prominent, but didn't detract a single ounce from her allure. He found himself wanting to know everything there was to know about her, from how she got the scar, to why she was living alone in the mountains, to how in the hell she'd gotten wrapped up with Remy fucking McCabe. But right now, one thing snared his curiosity more than all the others.

"What are you looking at?"

Amanda drew in a slow deep breath but didn't otherwise move. Finally, she blinked, eyes still on the window as her lips curled into a slow grin. "It's snowing."

Flicking a glance outside, Mason chuckled. "It's been snowing."

"No," she shook her head but didn't lift her chin from her palm. "It's *snowing* snowing," she informed.

Content to keep his focus on her, Mason had to force himself to turn and glance out the window. She was right. The sun had set fully, making the five pm hour feel like it was much later than he expected. What he didn't expect was the fat flakes of snow drifting silently down to earth. There were many different kinds of snow in Montana, but this one was his favorite. Fat flakes fell slower than most, making it feel like time had slowed. With the fall of night, the streets had died down and now, as the heavy snow silently blanketed everything like a quiet mother tucking her children in for the night, Mason felt cocooned, trapped in a tiny snow globe with just himself and Amanda. The restaurant had emptied too, and sitting in the dim light of the restaurant surrounded by warmth, with food filling his belly, and Amanda's presence soothing his inner beasts in a way nothing had in a long time, Mason had to admit that everything felt almost okay for once. He almost felt *peaceful*. Even if just for this brief moment, he found himself actually relaxing. The ever present knot that twisted his guts had loosened some time during dinner and honestly, he liked it. It was nice to concentrate on something besides the ever-present single-minded focus of finding his sister. It's all he'd thought on for years and he couldn't remember the last time she'd been placed at the back of his mind. His jaw ticked and he clenched his jaw against the bite of guilt that suddenly hit.

It vanished when the waiter returned with a bottle and asked, "More wine?"

Amanda looked from the waiter to Mason expectantly and he felt himself sit a little straighter. She was deferring to him, relying on him to make the decision for her, and holy shit! That unspoken gift of ownership, of taking control for her had his balls drawing up and his mouth suddenly going dry. Glancing at the waiter, he wondered if the man thought Amanda was his. He hoped the waiter thought she was with him. Eyes going back to Amanda, Mason could tell by the spark in her eye as she glanced at the bottle of wine that she was enjoying herself, so he immediately gestured toward her glass. "Please."

The waiter filled up Amanda's glass and inquired if Mason wanted more coffee. He declined and shooed the waiter away, wanting to watch Amanda's delight. His eyes didn't leave her as she sighed contentedly and took a drink from her wine, her attention given back to the snow. Her almost giddy behavior had him asking, "You come here often?"

Shaking her head, Amanda's eyes slid to his. "No. I've driven by a few times and have always wanted to come, but…"

"But what?"

Her smile faltered, and she looked down, shielding her face. She shook her head again and shrugged dismissively, but Mason wanted to know.

"But what?"

Angling her face back toward the window, Amanda admitted, "It's pretty expensive."

Her admission felt like a gut punch because while the restaurant was nice, it wasn't even close to being one of the fanciest in the small town. In fact, the prices on the menu hadn't been exorbitant or even slightly inflated. It had Mason shuffling through his memory of the files he'd just read on Amanda. He knew she was teaching at some rural school that was too far out for her to be driving during a Montana winter in an unreliable truck. He also knew that the cabin in the Highwoods had been bequeathed by her father upon his passing. What didn't make sense was her life prior to moving into her father's cabin. Amanda had a degree in Mathematics that she hadn't been using. She'd been a working as an administrative assistant for a financial service holding company here in town, but why? She could have been doing so much more.

He asked, "Do you like teaching?"

The question had Amanda's eyes narrowing on him. "I didn't tell you I was a teacher."

Busted. Shit!

Chapter 9

Amanda couldn't remember the last time she'd had such a splendid meal. The steak had been cooked to perfection and topped with grilled mushrooms and blue cheese crumbles, and the potato had been stuffed with butter, sour cream, bacon bits, and chives. And the wine had been the perfect touch. The restaurant was just as good as she had always thought it would be. What wasn't good was Mason's little slip. Taking a sip of her wine, she let it warm her suddenly chilled blood as she studied Mason and waited. He knew she was teaching? How?

Sitting up straighter, Mason's gaze didn't falter. His look was direct when he admitted. "I'm not going to lie. I looked into you."

The admission was disconcerting.

"Why?" she demanded.

"I need to know all I can about you, if I'm going to make amends."

"You don't need to make amends." Setting her glass down, she felt the contents of her stomach curdle and hated the sudden change of mood. She felt the pleasantness of dinner slipping away. "You can pay my medical bills and we'll be even."

The waiter arrived with the bill and Mason sent him off with a credit card, his eyes intent on Amanda the entire time.

"It displeases you that I looked into you?"

"Yes," she snapped. "I'm not a homework assignment. I'm not a project, Mason. I'm a person, and a private one at that." She felt her cheeks flaming the more she talked because the more she thought on it, the more she wondered what his snooping had uncovered. Her life was her business and no one else's.

"I just wanted to know about you," he tried to explain, but Amanda didn't want to hear anymore.

Shoving her chair back, she grabbed her purse and clipped out, "I need to use the restroom." Stalking away, she could feel Mason's eyes on her as she sucked back inexplicable tears. He'd looked into her. So what. *So what?* she self-admonished. She didn't need anybody digging up a past that she'd long since buried.

In the bathroom, she paced angrily, trying to calm herself down. All Mason would find—depending on how far back he went—would be the life of a lonely girl who'd been raised by a single mother until adulthood, when her mother died suddenly. Amanda had never known her father and honestly, she'd hated the man for abandoning them the way he had. He'd sent her letters after her mother's death, but she'd returned them all, and when she received word that he'd passed too, she'd never gotten over the guilt of ignoring his attempts at reconciliation. It wasn't that childish behavior that she was worried about Mason discovering though. It was the pattern of abandonment that plagued her. Mom had died, dad had died, and every man she'd ever dated had left her too. Something was wrong with her, and she didn't want Mason—or anyone—knowing that.

Stopping in front of the mirror, she stared at her reflection. People often told her she was pretty, but she didn't see it. All she saw was dark circles under eyes set in a too pale face and a scar through her brow that dominated nearly everyone's attention when they looked at her. Tearing her eyes away, she dragged in a steadying breath before throwing her shoulders back and lifting her chin. She wasn't going to let Mason rattle her. He hadn't earned that right.

Exiting the bathroom, she walked casually back into the restaurant and right up to the table. Mason stood as she approached. He gestured toward her glass of unfinished wine. "I've paid if you're ready to hit the road. Unless you'd like to finish your drink first."

With a sharp shake of her head, Amanda headed for the door, aware of Mason's presence closely behind her.

On the ride back to the Highwood Mountains the air in the car was thick, the oppressive weight of it pressing down on Amanda until she fidgeted in her seat uncomfortably.

Mason finally broke the silence. "I just wanted to know the basics, Amanda. I wasn't snooping just for the sake of it."

Face angled toward her window, she gritted out, "You could have just asked."

"I like to come into my battles prepared."

Head turning, she shot him a scathing look. "Is that what I am to you? A battle?"

With a slow shake of his head, he swallowed and looked almost repentant at the word. "I just meant…"

"I know what you meant." Amanda hugged her purse close to her stomach, almost like a shield as she stared straight ahead at the snow drifting over the road in the harsh wind that had slowly picked up the closer to the mountains they got. "I'm not your responsibility, Mason, and I don't want you feeling guilty over what happened. I'd appreciate you helping to chop my wood if you can, and some help with the medical expenses would be great, but I can take care of everything else. I'm no man's burden."

His voice was tight when he clipped out, "I didn't say you were, and I wasn't implying it either."

"Just stop," Amanda breathed, letting her head fall back against the head rest as she turned her body toward the window and stared out at the snow-covered prairie. "It's been a long day and I probably drank more wine than I should have considering the medication I'm on. I don't want to fight with you. I'm done fighting for the day. I'm just…done."

Chapter 10

Amanda's confession was doing all sorts of crazy shit to Mason's head. Glancing at her, he felt guilt for how tired she smelled and for how defeated she looked. It *had* been a long day, made even worse by the realization that he'd slipped up and allowed her to drink while on medication? What a dumb-dick move. How could he have forgotten that? How? It was easy when he'd felt like he was gifting her something by shucking convention and ordering white wine with dinner just to please her. Nostrils flaring, he drew her scent deeper and picked it apart. She was more than just simply tired. She was exhausted. It was the kind of exhaustion that came not just from physical fatigue, but from being emotionally drained too. He wondered if his admission of looking into her past played a part in that or if it was just the humiliation of having to deal with that wanker from the repair shop. And now an all new form of guilt was plaguing him. It had his hands gripping the steering wheel tightly as he glared at the road. Why did this woman have the to ability to make him feel so goddamn guilty all the time? It had him shooting her some scathing side eye that vanished the instant Amanda heaved a weighty sigh and let her head fall against the window. He felt that sigh all the way to his bones. He knew that type of fatigue intimately, and he didn't wish it on anyone.

"I'm sorry," he began, but Amanda quickly shut him down.

"Please don't. I don't want any more apologies, I don't wanna talk. I don't wanna think."

Slicing his gaze to her, he could only see one side of her face and saw that her eyes were closed.

"Let's just drive, okay?"

It was fine by him. The only thing he wanted to do was get Amanda out of his car, out of his nose, out of his head.

The drive proved to be longer than usual due to the storm and the low visibility on the road thanks to the blowing snow. Amanda's breathing had evened out shortly out of Great Falls and Mason had turned the heat to high to make sure she stayed toasty as she dozed in the passenger seat.

When they finally hit the Highwood mountains, all the relief that was supposed to come with nearly having Amanda home vanished when he wondered how in the hell she'd manage alone. By morning there'd be several feet of snow and in her current state, Amanda couldn't shovel, couldn't chop wood, and probably couldn't even stack wood in her damn hearth for a fire. Brows spearing down, Mason thought on all the things that'd need to be done tonight just to make her cabin livable for the evening. He felt a responsibility to help with those chores since he was the prat who'd encouraged her to order wine when he should have known she was on medication.

Maneuvering his car up the mountain path, he knew that if he needed to leave the Estate any time soon, he'd most likely have to borrow one of the Estate Humvees. While his Challenger was an all-wheel-drive, it'd be no match for the amount of snow the sky was promising. That had him thinking about Amanda. What would she do if something happened in the middle of the night? What if she had an emergency and there was no way for her to get to town?

Frustrated that he was slowly painting himself into a corner, he did something born of total desperation. Focusing, he concentrated to use the mystic—a telepathic means of communication for Skin Walkers—seeking out one Remy McCabe.

The attempt at connection went unanswered, so by the time Mason pulled his car to a stop in front of Amanda's cabin, he glared at the place for long minutes deciding whether he was staying with her or if he was taking her up to StoneCrow Estates. While he preferred the latter, he opted to stay at Amanda's place with her for two reasons. The first being that he didn't know if she had pets. Humans liked to keep small creatures in their homes and those animals relied on their humans for sustenance and warmth, and while he'd never scented any animals on Amanda, that didn't mean anything. One of the classrooms on the first floor of the manor at the Estate housed a habitat for dwarf hamsters and they didn't have much of a smell. Glancing at a still-sleeping Amanda, Mason tried to picture her cooing down at one of the two-inch furry creatures.

The second reason he opted for Amanda's cabin instead of the luxury of the Manor was because she'd mentioned medication and Mason wasn't sure if she carried it on her or if it was in her cabin someplace.

Staring at her, he snorted a quiet laugh.

Yeah, get her home and get away from her is really working well for me.

Carefully, Mason lifted Amanda's purse from her lap and opened it to fish around for her keys. Palming them, he quietly got out and made his way in the knee-deep snow to her cabin.

Inside Amanda's cabin, Mason made quick work of flicking on lights and starting a fire. The place was small, but clean, and cold as hell. The cold didn't bother him because he was a shifter and could regulate his temperature easily, but Amanda was a different story. In her bedroom, he found a baseboard heater set to low and cranked it up to high before searching the bathroom, living room, and kitchen for other heaters. She only had two. The one in the bedroom and one in the bathroom, which meant the main room would have to slowly be heated by the fire.

Shit!

Mason could almost see his breath and wondered what Amanda did on the days she had to work at that far off school. Glancing at her sink, he wondered how she kept her pipes from freezing and went to investigate. The tap was running ever so slightly and looking under the cupboard, Mason saw that her pipes were insulated. Still, it got arctic in these mountains and she needed actual heat.

Making a mental note to look into propane or gas heat, he headed out the front door to retrieve Amanda now that her cabin was set up as best it could be.

The purr of the motor was the only sound in the quiet night. He'd left it running to keep Amanda warm, and was now regretting it because it'd make it all the more colder once he got her out of the car.

Opening the passenger side door, he propped an arm on it as he ducked his head. "Amanda?"

She didn't stir.

"Amanda," he said more loudly. "You're home."

Still nothing.

Lowering a hand to shake her, his fingers stilled mid-air. Where did you grab a woman to shake her awake? The shoulder made the most sense, but the arm closest to him was the one in the sling. Bending lower, his hand was nearly to her thigh when he stopped. Eyes on her thigh, he realized how inappropriate touching her there would be.

Awww, bloody hell!

Bending low, he slid an arm behind Amanda's shoulders and then one beneath her knees before he lifted her effortlessly from the car. Half expecting her to startle awake, he was surprised when she snuggled into his chest. The move had his heart suddenly pounding too quickly. Nostrils flaring, he breathed in Amanda's scent. Her head was pressed into his shoulder and with just a slight turn of his jaw, his nose was brushing against the satiny softness of her dark hair. She smelled good, like pears. He loved pears. Just the thought of sinking his teeth into one and then using his tongue to lap at the juices had his dick going hard when the image suddenly shifted to one of Amanda laying bare before him, legs parted and head thrown back as he buried his face between her thighs.

The imagery had his head jerking forward with the realization of how inappropriate the thought was. A defenseless woman was passed out from sheer exhaustion in his arms and here he was thinking the most carnal of thoughts about her. Shame seared him as he lumbered through the snow toward the cabin.

Inside the cabin, he used his foot to kick the door closed before carrying Amanda to her bedroom. It was the warmest spot in the small cabin. Settling her in the middle of the bed, he quickly unlaced and peeled off her boots before covering her with the quilt folded at the foot of the bed. It was all he trusted himself to do before he went into her bathroom and dug around in the cabin and drawers for her medication. He didn't find it, but what he did find was a box hidden in the far back of a drawer. It was a home pregnancy test, and it was opened.

Glancing over his shoulder into Amanda's room, his lips thinned as he studied her sleeping form. Remy should be here right now. Not him.

Replacing the box and heading back into Amanda's room, he saw an orange bottle on her nightstand. Her meds. Going to the kitchen, he filled up a glass of water, checked the heaters in the bathroom and bedroom and stacked a few more logs on the fire before quietly letting himself out of Amanda's cabin.

That pregnancy test had given him an abrupt change of heart where caring for Amanda was concerned. Yeah, he'd fucked up her arm, but she wasn't his to care for or protect. She belonged to that douche Remy, and he'd make sure Remy did his damn job.

Chapter 11

Amanda woke not certain of where she was. Blinking into the darkness, it took a moment to recognize her own bedroom. Glancing at the window, she saw it was still dark and wondered what had awakened her. Taking a quick scan of her body, she realized the typically throbbing pain in her arm was only minimal, so that wasn't it.

Thump, thump, thump.

The noise drew her attention to her bedroom door. Was Mason still here? And if so, what in the hell was that noise?

Tossing the comforter off her legs, Amanda was relieved to find herself still fully clothed. She didn't remember making it home last night and wondered how she'd even gotten inside. Mason had to have carried her. *God how humiliating.*

Thump, thump, thump.

Opening her bedroom door, the front room was dark except for the small fire burning in the hearth.

Amanda called out, "Mason?"

The only answer was more thumping coming from the front door. It sounded almost like a muffled knock. The sound had fear-filled adrenaline flooding her. What if someone had gotten caught out in the storm, she could hear blustering outside?

Rushing to the door, Amanda jerked it open, but no one was there. Staring out into the swirling storm of wind and snow as arctic air blasted her overheated cheeks, she held up her good hand to block the wind as she squinted out into the night and yelled, "Hello! Is anyone out there!"

Ears straining for a response, she heard none. Looking down to see if there were footprints in the snow, she was shocked to find…blood!

With a startled gasp, Amanda jerked back, eyes shooting up from the ground to scan the darkness again. Inching the door closed, something in her periphery caught her attention and when she turned her head to look, she found a dead fox hanging by a rope that was nailed into her door.

Holy shit!

Living up in the mountains alone meant she wasn't squeamish in the least, but clearly someone had done this!

Giving one last look out into the darkness, she slammed the door and bolted it before rushing to flip on all the lights in the cabin and checking to make sure all her windows were locked. Her hands were shaking by the time she retrieved her shotgun from where she kept it leaned against the wall beside her nightstand. Double-checking to ensure it was loaded, she spun in a slow circle feeling the eerie press of fear and its clammy grip as she swallowed hard and remained as silent as possible, listening.

All she heard was the wind whipping outside the window. It sent the fox carcass to thumping against her door again, and unsure what to do, she scanned her bedroom for her purse. She found it on a chair near the door and had to set her shotgun on the bed before she hurried to her purse and pulled her cell free. Grateful it wasn't completely dead, she touched the icon that would connect her to the operator at StoneCrow Estates.

The phone rang twice before a feminine voice declared, "Stone Crow Estates."

"Mason EnemyHunter, please."

The line fell silent a moment before the receptionist asked, "May I tell him who's calling?"

"Amanda."

The line fell silent again like the receptionist was waiting for a last name, and when none was forthcoming, she clipped out, "One moment."

There was a clicking sound and then the line was ringing again. Finally, a groggy male voice answered, "Amanda? What's wrong?"

Angry now, Amanda had to suck back stinging tears of rage as she hissed, "Stay away from my cabin, Mason. I fucking mean it! You nailed a dead animal to my front door? It's just sick. Your jokes aren't funny. They're border-line cruel and..." She didn't want to have to make the threat, but he'd left her no choice. "If I have to tell Remy about this, then you'll be dealing with him!" She hung up before Mason could respond.

Hands still shaking, Amanda frowned at her phone and considered calling or texting Remy, but what was the point? He'd been avoiding her now for weeks. Still, Mason's little prank was uncalled for and outright mean.

Dropping onto her bed, Amanda pulled the shotgun until it rested across her thighs. Phone still in hand, she frowned at it for long minutes trying to decide if she wanted to try to reach out to Remy or not. The longer she thought on it, the more pissed she grew. If he wasn't serious about a relationship with her, he should have left her the hell alone!

Angry and growing more and more agitated with each thump of the fox against her door, Amanda shoved up from the bed and stomped to the front door. Without hesitation, she jerked the door open and glared out into the darkness. Leaning her shotgun just inside the door, she shouted out into the storm, "Thanks for the fresh meat!"

Reaching up, she unhooked the fox's noose from the nail it was wrapped around. Looking out into the dark, she flashed a merciless smile that didn't reflect in her eyes. And just to show she wasn't afraid, she lingered in the door longer than she wanted to, just a few solid minutes to prove her point. That point being that she wouldn't be intimated by Mason or Remy or anyone else for that matter.

Stepping back inside, she slammed the door closed and then fell back against it as her breathing turned ragged. The rope slipped from her fingers and the frozen fox hit the floor with a dull thud.

Why would Mason play such a cruel prank? It had to be him. He was the last one at her cabin and had taken advantage of her unconscious state to be mean. Was he mad he'd had to deal with the jerk at the garage for her and then give her a ride back? Was he upset about having to pay for her dinner? Or was he just an asshole, like Remy. She was starting to see a pattern with male Skin Walkers and it wasn't a favorable one.

Shoving up off the floor with her good arm, she snagged the rope and carried the fox to the sink. She didn't want it inside because she knew it most likely had fleas. It was difficult stuffing the fox into a garbage sack before she shoved the sack into her freezer to be dealt with later.

She was walking tiredly back toward the front door to retrieve her shotgun when the door suddenly exploded open. Amanda screamed and stumbled backward, her hand going up to block her eyes from the snow that blasted into the living room. Squinting through the whipping wind and stinging snowflakes, she could make out a large figure dominating the doorway. Heart in her throat, she didn't know whether to scream or run.

Chapter 12

"Amanda!"

It took Amanda two seconds to recognize Mason's voice, and then her fear shifted quickly to outrage.

"What in the hell are you doing?" she raged taking a small step toward him. "I told you to stay the hell away!"

As he stormed into the cabin, Mason brushed her shoulder as he passed, his eyes going everywhere. "Whose blood is that on the porch? What in the bloody hell is going on? Who's here?"

"Who's here?" she mocked. "You know what you did. Now leave!" Jamming a finger toward the door, she waited, but Mason didn't even glance at her. Instead, he disappeared into her room.

Following close behind, Amanda barked. "Leave, Mason. Now!" She glared at him as he made a show of checking her bathroom and closet. "Did you hear me?"

Mason stalked passed her, heading back out to the main room as he clipped out, "Pack a bag. You're not staying here."

"The hell I'm not," Amanda seethed on his heels.

In front of her, Mason stopped so abruptly that she would have collided with his back had he not spun inhumanly fast and caught her. Eyes intent as he stared down at her, Mason's tone was matter of fact when he informed. "It wasn't me."

His admission knocked the air from her lungs. "Wh-what?"

"I didn't leave that...*prize* on your door." Releasing her, he plowed a hand through his hair as he eyed the main room a moment before dropping his arm and hurrying to where her coat hung on a hook near the door. "But I appreciate your vote of confidence."

His tone was mocking and would have normally incited a snarky remark, but Amanda was too confused to respond. Her mind was reeling. If Mason hadn't been messing with her, then who was?

Remy?

Now that she thought on it, it did seem more Remy's style. Where Mason was always brooding and serious, Remy was more carefree and playful, almost to a fault. In fact, every time in the past when Amanda had been on the verge of ending her relationship with Remy, he'd tease, pester, and plead her into giving him one more chance.

Watching Mason gather her coat and boots, Amanda sighed. "I'm not leaving. It's just Remy messing around."

Mason stilled and shot her an incredulous look. "By pinning a dead animal to your door in the middle of the night?"

Shrugging up her good arm, Amanda looked at the floor. "He has a weird sense of humor."

Mason's eyes bulged. "A weird sense of hu…" Shaking his head, he started pacing, mumbling to himself, but Amanda picked up his words. "What a sick, twisted fuck." Stopping, he pinned her with a hard look, jamming his finger at the door. "That shit's not funny."

She agreed, but instead of admitting that she just shrugged her good shoulder again. "I'm used to it."

"Then why call me?" Mason thundered, planting his hands on his lean, jean-clad hips.

In the faded denim and tight-fitting white t-shirt, it was one of the few times, Amanda had seen Mason dressed so casually. With his shirt clinging to his muscled torso, she couldn't help but admit that he looked hot. Really hot.

"Amanda!" Mason prodded almost angrily. "Why accuse me? If Remy does this kind of shit all the time, why call me?"

Turning her back on him, she padded to the couch and dropped down on it. Lifting her hand to her forehead, she scrubbed that hand wearily down her face, pinching her eyes closed. "I'm tired. I...panicked."

When she opened her eyes, Mason was standing in front of her, hands still on his hips and a smirk on his face. "So, you panicked and thought of *me* first?"

"*Accused* you first," she clarified shoving to her feet and shooting him side-eye as she skirted the couch and headed back to her room. "Turn off the lights when you leave."

"Amanda."

She ignored him and went into her room, flipping the door closed behind her and flicking off the lights as she made her way to the bed. Before she could even settle fully onto the mattress, the light clicked back on and there Mason stood. Leaned up against the door frame, arms crossing over a broad chest and bicep muscles bulging, he shot Amanda an annoyed look. "Pack some shit. You're not staying here."

With a delicate snort, Amanda settled into bed and made a show of pulling the comforter up over her slinged arm and just beneath her chin before laying her good arm atop the covers. "Lights off on your way out."

She didn't hear Mason move so her eyes startled open when the blanket around her tightened and she was lifted off the bed. Arms trapped inside the blanket, all she could do was squirm and yell, "Hey! Put me down!"

"Stop," Mason commanded on a growl. "You'll hurt your bad arm. Be still."

"Be still?" Amanda asked then asked again on a near hysterical shrill. "What are you even doing?" she snapped. "You gonna carry me all the way to StoneCrow. I didn't hear your car pull up outside!"

***

Christ, Amanda was right. What *was* he doing?

Standing with her in his arms, Mason's surge of adrenaline was just now starting to wear off, but the imperative need to protect her hadn't lessened in the slightest.

"You can't stay here," he grumbled, looking around the front room of her cabin in hopes of finding a solution for his dilemma. Amanda was right, he'd shifted and flown to her cabin, which meant his car was still parked back at the estate. And with Amanda's truck still in the shop, there was no way to get her to StoneCrow.

"Take me back to my room," Amanda griped. "It was a false alarm. You're overreacting."

Was he? He didn't feel like he was overreacting, and the thought of taking Amanda back to her bed and leaving without her felt like underreacting. To push the point home, he growled, "Your phone call didn't sound like an overreaction." Glancing down, he saw her cheeks flame before she angled her face away from him. Her jaw worked in anger and he knew why. Any reasoning she gave for the phone call would only prove his point. She called because beneath all her bravado and anger had been fear. He wasn't about to punish her for doing the right thing though, and that was odd. His typical gratification at being right was oddly absent.

Turning, he carried Amanda back to her room and settled her on the bed.

"Thank you," she muttered quietly, adjusting her blankets around her. "Please make sure you lock the door when you leave."

"I'm not leaving."

"Well you're not staying," she countered, but Mason was already seated on the edge of the bed, bent over, and unlacing his boots.

"Mason," she griped. "It was a joke. Just someone fooling around."

"A dead animal nailed to your door isn't a joke. And if it was meant to be, it was a sick and twisted one." Toeing off his shoes, he sat upright and looked over his shoulder at her. "Tell me again why you thought it was me."

With a roll of her eyes, Amanda sighed wearily. "You were the last one here. The only person who's been here in weeks." She shrugged. "Just made sense."

Sliding off the bed, Mason extended his legs in front of him and pressed his shoulders into the mattress behind him. Arms crossing over his chest, he frowned at the bedroom door. "For the record, I don't get my kicks out frightening women."

"Yeah," Amanda snorted. "Just hurting them."

Chapter 13

As soon as the words were out, Amanda regretted them. Her shame only heightened when Mason's shoulders tensed.

"Sorry," she muttered. "I don't know why I said that."

"I do," he clipped out, his tone emotionless as he stayed seated on the floor facing the door. "I *did* hurt you. It was an accident and one I've never truly apologized for."

"You don't have..."

He cut her off. "I'm sorry, Amanda." Turning, he gave her his profile, but didn't look at her. "What I did was unforgivable. Inexcusable, and something I can't explain. An apology seems so insufficient."

"It was an accident."

"Was it?" he asked. Facing the door again, he muttered, "Why you?" Then almost to himself he continued more quietly, "I've been so distracted for so long. Startled out of a reverie by countless people." Sniffing, he lifted his chin and spoke more loudly. "So why when you touched me did I lose it? It was like I had zero control."

Amanda focused on the ceiling. "You were taken by surprise. That's all." But she could tell by the frown she caught on his face when she glanced at him as he shook his head that he didn't believe it.

"It doesn't matter now," she offered. "What's done is done. Your apology is accepted. Go to sleep or go home, Mason."

Rolling on her side away from him, she ended the conversation and struggled for what felt like forever to fall asleep. The fact that Mason remained in the room, seated on the floor beside the bed, made the task damn near impossible, but sleep did come. Brief as it was.

Amanda stirred from her slumber, unsure what had woken her. In the darkened room, she heard a rustling and her heart rate spiked from a practical stall to a million miles an hour.

"Easy," a masculine voice crooned in the dark. "Just adjusting my body."

Amanda instantly recognized the voice but had to be sure. "Mason?"

"Yeah. It's just me."

"You're still here?"

He chuffed a quiet laugh. "Obviously."

"Why aren't you on the couch?"

He didn't respond and feeling a bite of guilt, Amanda asked, "You want the bed? I can take the couch."

"No, I don't want your bed. I wouldn't be able to handle that."

What does that mean? Still blinking the sleepy fog from her brain, Amanda wasn't sure she'd heard him correctly. When she replayed the words and realized she had heard him right, she wanted to know what the words meant.

Before she could ask, Mason bit out a tired sounding, "I can't sleep. My animals are still riled up from thinking you were in danger."

Unsure how to respond, Amanda offered a timid, "S-sorry?"

"Don't be sorry. There's nothing for you to apologize for. Just...talk to me," he commanded, fishing into his pocket and pulling out the locket with the black and white baby picture of his sister. It was the only thing he had of her, the only evidence that she even existed. It was the lone single memento Monroe's Sentries had been able to dig up after they'd raided the Megalya facility where Mason and his sister's parents were held and tortured. Smoothing his fingers over the soft gold that had worn down with time and his constant attention, Mason felt something in him settle. The locket always soothed him, it anchored him. Clicking it opened he glanced down at his sister's picture. She was it, the only blood relative he had left, but at least he had that. Many Walkers were alone, or never got to know their parents or siblings before they were terminated.

Shoving up to a sitting position, Amanda lifted her hands and scrubbed them down her face before raking her fingers through her scalp. "Whose picture is in there?" she asked, her tone almost hostile.

It had Mason clicking the locket closed and shoving it back into his pocket.

"Your wife? A girlfriend? An ex?"

With a snort, he sighed deeply, prepared not to answer.

"If your so worried about her, you can go."

At Amanda's heightened ire, Mason turned his head and shot her a look.

"What?" she snapped. "I don't want to be the one to break up a happy marriage or wreck a family. If you have a woman waiting, you should go see her."

"It's my sister," he bit out tersely, not wanting to discuss his sibling, but unwilling to have Amanda thinking he was with her and pining for someone else. Which in and of itself was interesting. He'd never cared before what people thought of his preoccupation with the locket, or rather, the picture nestled inside. But for some reason, it mattered now. What Amanda thought mattered.

"Sister?" Amanda asked. "She live up at StoneCrow too?"

"No."

Silence reigned before Amanda demanded, "Well what? Where is she?"

Agitation growing, Mason clipped out, "Missing. She's been missing since birth. I've never met her. But I'll never stop looking."

"Jesus," Amanda breathed. "I'm...I'm so sorry. I can't imagine how that must feel. You've gotta be..."

"Talk about you," Mason commanded, wanting to change the subject. "Tell me about this place. How'd you end up living out here in this cabin all alone?"

Silence reigned again and he knew Amanda was considering if she wanted to allow him this shift in topic. After a few moments, Amanda heaved a reluctant sigh. "It was my dad's place."

It was all she offered, so Mason pushed, "*And*...he gave it to you?"

"He *left* it to me."

"I'm sorry," Mason offered sincerely.

"Don't be. He wasn't a good man. Not worthy of my sorry, let alone anyone else's."

***

In the dark, Mason could see clearly through his animals' sight. Angling his head, he slid his gaze to Amanda. The room was pitch black and she had no idea he was studying her. It left her vulnerable in a way she wouldn't be if she knew he could see her. She was sitting up in bed, arms crossed over her lap as she rocked back and forth. She was trying to sound relaxed, disinterested, but the firm set to her jaw, the rigidity of her shoulders gave her away.

"We don't have to talk about him," he offered.

"It's fine," Amanda bit out a little too curtly. With an explosive sigh, she started, "He was a total fuck. He wasn't loyal to my mom, and he was abusive."

That had Mason's hackles rising. There wasn't anything he despised more than a man who used his fists on women or children. It was the highest form of cowardice in his book.

"Not to me," Amanda admitted, extinguishing some of Mason's venom. "Just to my mom. He beat her up all the time."

Eyes glued to Amanda, Mason watched her lower lip tremble a moment before she sucked it into her mouth and bit on it a moment before offering one more word. "Bad."

That word had chills blasting up his arms. *How bad?* he wondered. Had Amanda been there, had she witnessed the abuse?

"One time, he beat her so badly she was unrecognizable. I screamed at him and begged him to stop."

Her story stalling a moment, Mason strained his ears in anticipation of what more she would offer, simultaneously wanting to know everything and nothing at all. His inner beasts certainly didn't want to hear more. They were already up, pacing just beneath the surface, lips peeled back, claws shooting out with the need to protect...to avenge. But the human part of Mason needed to hear more. He wanted to know what Amanda had endured. He needed to know what had driven a beautiful woman into the wilds of Montana to claim the cabin of a much despised father, and to do so alone.

The silence swelled between them, feeling almost tangible before Amanda continued.

"She was so bad after that beating that when she went to the courthouse to file for a divorce, the clerk took her back into the Judge's chambers. As soon as the Judge saw her, he signed the divorce on the spot. No hearing, no response to the filing from my father. He just signed it and apologized."

"And that was it?" Mason asked.

With a delicate snort, Amanda huffed a humorless sound. "I wish." Falling back onto the bed, Amanda blinked up at the ceiling and frowned hard. "You know it took me until just this year to realize my mom was just as much to blame as him. I mean, yeah, he was a monster, but she was the one who kept letting the monster in. After the divorce, he just kept coming back and even after that beating, she kept trying with him. She kept letting him come home and kept taking more beatings. Then he'd leave and run to the other woman and get bored or whatever and come back to Ma. Eventually he chose his mistress, and I was so damn happy. I thought we were finally done seeing him, but we weren't. It was like a nightmare you couldn't shake. He just kept coming back and leaving and coming back."

"That must have been so hard on you."

His words had Amanda's eyes slicing from the ceiling to look towards him. She couldn't see him in the dark, but he could read her expression easily. Confusion. She looked baffled, like she'd never even considered her own plight in all she'd endured.

Eyes going back to the ceiling, she muttered, "I guess."

She guessed? Pulling his feet in, Mason sat cross-legged on the floor, scooting until his back was pressed into the wall and he was facing her. "What do you mean, you guess? You don't know if it was hard on you?"

Brows furrowing, her lips thinned before she clipped out, "I was a kid. I'm sure it would have been hard on any child."

"Ain't asking about any child, Amanda." Her dismissiveness of what must have been a horrendous childhood made him inexplicably angry. "I'm asking about you."

"What is this," she snorted. "Therapy?" With a roll of her eyes she changed the subject. "What about you? What are you doing out here? From your accent, this isn't your real home."

But Mason wasn't having it. "Uh-uh," he shook his head. "We're not done talking about you."

Amanda's brows snapping down almost made him want to chuckle.

"Finish your story," he ordered.

Amanda rolled her head to the side to glare in his general direction.

"You said your dad left you this place." Mason looked around the cabin. "But if you didn't like him and he disappeared on you and your mom, then why are you here? Why accept the gift of this place?"

As soon as he asked, Amanda's eyes slammed closed, but even with them closed he saw her complexion go stark. Her jaw clenched like she was gnashing her teeth against something she didn't want to say, and her brows furrowed just a little deeper. He didn't know why but seeing her reaction to the question had him regretting even asking. He was about to change the subject entirely when Amanda finally turned her head away from him and opened her eyes. "Mom moved on," she started quietly. "She remarried and started a new life, but the older I got, the more curious I grew about *him*. I mean there had to be something good in him for her to be with him in the first place. Some redeeming quality. She hung onto him for a long time, hoping he'd change his mind and choose her, choose *us*. She pined for him a long time. But why?"

Rolling her head back toward him, Amanda looked genuinely confused when she asked, "Why would she do that?"

Mason didn't have an answer, so he stayed silent.

"He hit her more than he ever kissed her. He lied to her more than he ever told the truth. He was...was...a giant piece of shit! But she still wanted him."

Mason watched as Amanda's eyes pooled with tears.

"I wished I would have asked her before, when it was still relevant, but bringing it up to her now would feel like raining on her parade." Amanda sighed heavily and lifted her good hand to rub absently at her slinged arm. "When he died and I got the letter saying he left me his place, I felt compelled to come up here and try to figure him out."

"What about the other woman?" Mason glanced around quick. "Did she live here with him too?"

Amanda shrugged. "Nah. He wasn't good to her either so apparently, she ran as fast and as far as she could. If she'd still been around, I'd have let her have this place."

"No animosity?"

"Nah," Amanda shook her head sadly. "She didn't owe us loyalty. He did. He was the one that fucked up our lives. Not her. In fact, she really did Ma a favor. I couldn't imagine how miserable she would have been if they'd stayed together?" More quietly she muttered, "He probably would have eventually killed her."

Feeling a gamut of emotions, none of which were pleasant, Mason finally bit out, "Why are you here, Amanda?"

"At first I told myself that I wanted to see the purgatory where he'd wound up." Sitting up again, she pooled the blankets around her hips as she stared into the darkness almost like it was easier to speak when you didn't have to look at anyone. "I'd hoped he was in some hellhole, living off cans of spam, and regretting his horrible choices. I wished he was missing mom, missing her cooking and cleaning, and her taking care of him. I wished he was miserable out in the world missing us and regretting how bad he'd been. But..." She fell silent a moment before she admitted, "This place isn't that bad. I mean winters are hard as hell, but summers up here..."

She didn't have to tell him. Mason already knew. Summers in Montana were the Creator's gift to those rare souls who braved some of the harshest winters imaginable. Montana summers were hard fought for and heavenly.

"It's actually beautiful up here. If it weren't for the loneliness, it'd be perfect."

That admission had Mason's eyes narrowing on her. And now he had to ask. "You and Remy..."

"Don't!" she sighed, flinging herself back on the bed. "Just don't." Rolling onto her side away from him she bit out, "It's late. Couch is all yours."

Jaw ticking, Mason stared at Amanda's back. He didn't like being so easily dismissed, but assumed he'd prefer it to listening to Amanda wax poetic about her and Remy's love life. And that thought was unsettling. Why should he care about listening to this woman talk about her lover? He shouldn't, but knew he would, so he shoved up off the floor and padded in socked feet out of the room, shooting Amanda one last glance with a mumbled, "Night," before he headed for the couch.

Tomorrow he'd get shit squared away. Amanda's truck, a job, a safe place to stay. Those three things were the least he could do for the damage he'd inflicted.

Hmmm, that had him thinking about her arm as his eyes dipped to where it rested outside the covers on Amanda's side. He'd get it looked at first thing in the morning when he got Amanda to StoneCrow Estates.

Chapter 14

Amanda fidgeted nervously under the commanding scrutiny of the one and only Monroe StoneCrow. Standing in his office beside Mason, Amanda felt like a child who'd been called to the principal's office. The absolute power exuding from Monroe was undeniable and had Amanda side-stepping by mere fractions to get closer to Mason. Mason noticed too because he shot her side-eye and then smirked.

Jerk!

Eyes roving her frame, Monroe offered, "Amanda, it's good to see you again."

She'd met him once when she and Remy had first started dating. It was just the briefest of encounters, a mere two seconds worth of introduction and nothing more, but even that had left her shaken. There was something about Monroe, something about the mantle of authority he carried that reminded her of a massive African lion prowling his kingdom.

Stifling the shiver that wanted to wash over her, she smiled woodenly. "Nice to see you too."

Monroe's assessing blue gaze narrowed on her slingless arm.

Beside her, Mason stiffened as he explained, "We visited Dr. Arkinson in the infirmary this morning."

Lifting a hand to press a finger into his lips, Monroe looked displeased as he stared pointedly at Mason and waited.

Mason cleared his throat and explained, "Since Ms. Chandler is in a relationship with one of our Sentries and is familiar with Walkers, I thought it'd be fine if we took care of her arm. Especially, since it was a Walker who injured her."

Lowering his hand, Monroe narrowed his eyes on Mason. "You."

"Yes."

Amanda glanced at Mason and watched his face his go red.

"Me," Mason continued. "I injured Ms. Chandler and since she's to be my assistant, I thought it best to have her healed fully."

"Those decisions are to be mine and mine alone," Monroe chastised and then dismissed the subject with a lift of his hand, when Mason opened his mouth to argue. Intense gaze sliding from

Mason to Amanda, Monroe said, "I've been informed that you've been selected as Mason's new assistant."

It wasn't a question and Monroe's gaze shifted back to Mason so Amanda wasn't sure if she was supposed to respond or not. Mason saved her from the confusion when he answered for her.

"Yes," he clipped out. "She starts in the morning."

Glancing at him, Amanda noted that Mason's tone and demeanor seemed almost annoyed, confrontational at least. It didn't seem like the proper level of respect one should use when addressing a man like Monroe StoneCrow, so she leaned over and tried to unnoticeably shoulder bump Mason's arm. When he glanced down at her she gave him a stern look and then turned her attention back to Monroe.

"Yes...*sir*," she tagged on quickly. "If that's okay? I worked as an administrative assistant for a local financial service holding company. This won't be my first rodeo." Her confidence faltered as Monroe studied her a little too intently. "But this is happening really fast. If you want to hold off until you can check references..."

"He doesn't," Mason grunted.

"Or if you had someone else in mind for the position..."

Again, Mason bit out, "He doesn't."

Amanda shot Mason a quick dirty look and hissed a quiet, "Shhh." Eyes snapping back to Monroe, she started again, "I don't want to put anyone out or..."

"You're not!" Mason barked and earned himself another side-glare from Amanda.

"I apologize for Mason," she explained. "He spent half the night on the floor in my cabin and the other half on my too small sofa. He's just cranky."

Monroe's stern expression broke. His face split into a grin as a throaty chuckle escaped him. "Relegated to the floor, eh?" His penetrating gaze slid to Mason as he openly mocked, "Tsk, tsk, tsk."

Beside her, Mason tensed, and Amanda didn't understand what was happening.

Monroe chided, "You may not be aware of this, Ms. Chandler, but Mason is *always* cranky." He shot her a wink that had Amanda smiling gratefully.

Beside her, a deep growl rattled its way up Mason's throat.

Monroe shut it down quickly when his expression went hard, and his eyes slid to Mason. "Take her to a suite. Get her settled."

"Th-thank you," Amanda stuttered, confused. "But I don't need a place to stay. I have my cabin. I just need the job."

The sudden darkening of Monroe's expression had an eerie feeling creeping its way up Amanda's spine. It only intensified when he looked to Mason with a clearly reproachful expression, like there was something Mason had forgotten to tell her.

Sighing wearily, Monroe shook his head. "You work here, you stay here."

"But...I'm just down the mountain." Amanda pointed toward the window that overlooked the estate. "I can be here in under ten minutes."

Without looking down at her, Mason grouched, "Your truck's still in the shop."

Glaring up at him, Amanda gritted out, "I can walk here in twenty."

"No need to walk," Monroe cut in. "You'll stay in a suite. Problem solved."

Shoving up from his desk, Monroe gathered some papers and then turned his back on Amanda and Mason. The dismissal was irksome. No one was listening to her, and Amanda didn't appreciate being ignored.

Stepping toward Monroe, Amanda was stopped by Mason's hand on her arm, which she immediately shook off. "I don't *want* to stay here."

Her blood chilled when Monroe slowly turned to face her. He didn't speak. He didn't have to.

"No," Amanda bit out. "I don't have to stay here. I won't!" Turning, she strode determinedly for the door that led from Monroe's office. She'd been forced to tolerate a great deal since coming to Montana. She'd done what she had to do and begrudgingly accepted those things she had no choice but to endure, but this? Having her choices stripped from her completely? It wasn't happening.

She'd just jerked the door open and stormed out when the two towering Sentries who'd been planted on either side of the hall outside the door, caught her arms, forcing her to stop.

"Let me go," she seethed giving them each her best glare. It didn't accomplish a thing. "I-I'd like to leave," she stammered.

Still, the Sentries held firm. Turning her, they dragged her back into Monroe's office.

"Hey!" she yelled, but the Sentries ignored her. Pissed, she tried to plant her feet, but they just lifted her off the ground. Afraid they'd reinjure her newly healed arm, she bent her elbow and tried to pull that arm free with an alarmed, "Stop!"

"Take your fucking hands off her!" Mason snarled, rushing them.

Monroe roared, "Mason!" And when Mason kept right on heading for the Sentries, Monroe thundered, "Let her go!"

As soon as the Sentries released her, Amanda hurried to Mason who instantly pulled her into the safety of his arm. Panting against his chest, Amanda sucked back the sudden tears that threatened.

Above her, Mason challenged, "Must you make every interaction into a bloody war?"

Monroe snorted. "You asked for help. I gave it." He looked from Mason to Amanda. "Ms. Chandler, you need a place to stay, and I've provided that. You seek employment, it's been granted." Brows spearing down, he chastised, "Perhaps a little gratitude." When he pursed his lips and shot her a disapproving look, Amanda felt properly chastised.

With embarrassed heat flooding her cheeks, she tried to explain herself. "I'm sorry. I *am* grateful for your offer." She shot a look at the Sentries, "But there's a difference between being offered and being forced." Eyes going back to Monroe she continued, "It didn't feel like I had a choice about staying or not and that…"

Monroe cut her off, "You don't."

Falling silent, Amanda swallowed hard as her earlier fear returned. Head turning slowly, she looked up at Mason. She couldn't keep the tremble from her voice when she asked, "M-ason? What's going on?"

Mason was glaring at Monroe with a fury she hadn't witnessed before. It gave her hope that he'd surge to her defense, but it was Monroe who did all the talking.

"You signed a contract, Ms. Chandler."

Her attention shot back to him. "What?"

"When you first moved here, you signed a contract with me."

"I did no such thing! I only ever signed the paperwork signing my father's acreage over to me. He left it to me in his will."

"It was contested."

"What?" She shook her head, "What are you talking about?"

"He had a business partner. They were planning on starting an outfitting business for local hunters. When your father left the place to you in the will he had drafted, his partner objected. I stepped in and bought out both parties. I own your father's land. Out of consideration, I've been permitting you to stay there knowing it wouldn't be long term."

"What?" she breathed, unsure if he was telling the truth or not. "You're...you're lying. I have the paperwork."

That had Monroe's expression going dark. "I don't lie, Ms. Chandler." He rounded his desk and took a seat. "I don't have to."

"Then why would you let me stay there?" she challenged. "If it's yours, then *why*?"

He shrugged one shoulder negligently, his focus on a stack of papers in front of him as he took up his pen and answered simply, "Pity."

The word felt like a cold steel blade sinking into her stomach.

"Bloody hell," Mason breathed beside her. He released her and stormed up to Monroe's desk, slapping his palms onto the shiny surface as he leaned across it to snarl, "What is wrong with you? Have you no tact?"

Monroe slowly lifted his head. "You want the woman here for her safety? She's here. You're welcome." Eyes dipping back to his paperwork, Monroe dismissed them both with a flick of his fingers. "Now, if you don't mind."

Mason stood to his full height and turned to face Amanda. When he did, she wasn't sure what the apologetic look of defeat on his face meant.

"Mason?" she queried losing hope. "What does this mean?"

"It means you're staying," Monroe answered for him. "King, see Ms. Chandler to her suite. Ms. Chandler, I'll have Lilly bring you a copy of the legal work. You can review it at your leisure."

Pissed and scared, Amanda snarled, "I can't leave?" When no one answered she shouted, "I'm a prisoner then?"

The ass that he was, Monroe bounced his head from shoulder to shoulder in a tomato tomahto gesture before clipping out, "Let's use the word *guest*. Shall we?"

"Guests can go home," she snapped.

"I think we've already established that you have no home."

The admission made her suck in a sharp breath. Frustrated tears blinded her.

"Goddamn it, Monroe!" Mason snatched her hand and pulled her from the room.

Dazed, Amanda followed Mason blindly. Her steps felt wooden and she couldn't really focus as she replayed what had just happened. "Did...did I just lose my home?"

"No," Mason fumed, but his denial didn't feel true.

"How did this happen?" Amanda asked herself. "How could I not know?"

"He may be lying," Mason offered. "I'll look into it."

"But he doesn't lie," Amanda countered, being pulled along behind Mason. Her voice grew brittle when she repeated, "He doesn't have to."

Chapter 15

Sitting in his suite, frowning out the window at the dark night, Mason listened to the howling wind. With his heightened sense of hearing he could even pick up the slight pings of crystalline snowflakes blasting against the glass. Reaching for his rocks glass, he lifted it and absently swirled the amber Elijah Craig bourbon within until the warmed scent lifted and drew his attention back to the table where he sat. His lone place setting at the too long table in his suite never failed to remind him that he hadn't done his job. Eyeing the empty seats, he wondered how long it would be before his sister and any family she may have would finally be able to join him. Sighing, he forced down the quiet whisper of, "if ever." Tonight, he wasn't going to think about his sister or his failure of finding her thus far. Tonight, he was too distracted by something else. Focusing on the gold rimmed place setting before him, Mason lifted his matching gold spoon and stabbed it uninterestedly into the fisherman's pie still steaming on his plate. He couldn't recall how many nights he'd spent in this exact same spot eating and drinking the exact same thing. Angling his head, his eyes slid back to the window and he sighed, staring at the exact same sight. Before, this had been his favored end to an evening, but now it felt hollow. No, hollow wasn't the right word. Dropping his spoon, Mason laced his fingers together and propped them under his chin while dissecting his emotions. With a chuff of self-loathing, he lowered his hands as realization dawned. It wasn't hollowness he was feeling at all. What he was feeling was loneliness, and this time it wasn't for long lost family.

Shoving back from the table, Mason snatched up his glass of bourbon and stalked to the fireplace, silently cursing Amanda. She was fucking with his head, fucking with his routine. Even worse, she was distracting him from his goal of finding his sister. With that thought, guilt bit hard. His sister was out there, God knew where, and here he was wondering how Amanda was adjusting to her suite.

She's fine, he self-admonished.

Of course, Amanda was fine. She was safe in a suite just down the hall. The rooms at the Estate were impeccable and the service was first-class. Still, he couldn't stop the worry that plagued him. He'd delivered her to the suite himself, but she'd begged him to take her home. He'd practically shoved her inside and left her trapped there. Monroe had the automated locks engaged so that the only way for Amanda to be let out of her suite was for someone on the outside to allow it.

Trying not to think of Amanda, Mason headed for the leather armchair angled toward the warmly-lit fire. Dropping into it, he took a swig of his bourbon before placing it on a side table and opened the laptop on the ottoman in front of him. With an ease that spoke of years of repetition, he logged in and pulled up his encrypted files. His fingers flew over the keyboard as he studied documents he'd already read a dozen times, searching for anything he'd missed where the hunt for his sister was concerned. A flag drew him to his mail and the mountain of e-mails awaiting his attention. Clicking on anything that looked like a potential lead, he responded as needed, ignoring the tension in his shoulders.

An alert drew his attention to the top of his inbox, and when he opened Commander Conn Drago's e-mail, he had to do a double read. It was a quick response to an e-mail he'd just sent to the Commander.

This was the mission from two weeks ago. It was a dead end. You were briefed. You alright?

Slamming his laptop shut, Mason buried both hands in his hair and fell back into his chair. He couldn't fucking focus. He couldn't fucking eat! It seemed the only action he was capable of was thinking about Amanda Chandler and how she was adjusting to life in her new cell. She'd been more than upset when Monroe refused to let her leave. She'd been distraught and hurt. It was that hurt that had Mason pissed and still off kilter. It was so easy for everyone else on the Estate to be diplomatic, except for Monroe fucking StoneCrow!

Prick!

Monroe could have handled things better. He could have gotten Amanda to stay without her knowing there was no choice in the matter. But no! The Dominant seemed to gain pleasure from torturing people and flouting his power over them.

Standing, Mason eyed his rapidly cooling dinner and then looked at his closed laptop. He'd accomplish nothing if he didn't deal with Amanda first.

Bending, he grabbed his rocks glass and emptied it in one swallow before stalking toward the door, a man on a mission.

***

Lying on the couch, glaring at the curtained window, Amanda ignored the growling of her stomach. She was too angry to eat. She was too angry to do anything but sulk on the couch while tears slid silently from her eyes.

Not a captive. A guest! she mimicked inwardly, teeth grinding at Monroe's words. It wasn't just Monroe she was pissed at either. In her estimation, Mason shared at least half the blame for even bringing her here at all. He'd made it sound like things would be better. He'd made things sound too good to be true.

Rolling to her back, she swiped at her cheeks and sucked back her tears, now angry with herself for having been so goddamn naive for believing him.

A soft knock rapped on the door and she ignored it. She didn't want company.

Arms crossed over her chest, socked feet crossed at the ankles with one jerking back and forth in rapid agitation, she wondered how in the hell she was going to get off the Estate. She'd already tried the phone on the end-table beside the couch. It only took her to the Estate operator. As for her cell phone, taken.

A second knock had her stifling a growl as her eyes rolled to where the door was on the other side of the couch.

"Amanda?"

She recognized Mason's voice and said nothing. He hadn't lied to her, but she still felt tricked. She felt like he knew enough to know that Monroe owned her land. He had to know, right? As the Estate's Chief Financial Officer, it would be Mason's job to know what Monroe StoneCrow owned. And right now, it felt like Monroe owned her, and she hated it.

More tears slipped free and Amanda rolled to face the back of the couch. When she heard the keycard slot beep and the door squeak open, she grabbed the nearest throw pillow and used it to cover her face before gritting out, "Get out!"

"Are...are you crying?"

Mason's voice was right above her and his tone was filled with what sounded to be a cross between concern and fear.

"Get out, Mason!"

"No," he boomed then pulled the pillow from over her face. "Why are you crying?"

Burying her face in the couch, Amanda lost it and screamed out her frustration. "I said get the fuck out!"

Dumb man that he was, Mason not only refused to listen, he grabbed her and hauled her up like she was light as a doll.

Good and pissed, Amanda writhed in his hold, not caring if her dropped her or not. Hair full of static from when he'd ripped the pillow off her head, Amanda's flowing hair clung to everything, including her own face. She didn't care. One hand shoved at Mason's chest, putting space between them while she swung her other opened hand up for a well-deserved slap.

Mason dodged her hand like a pro and it only enraged her more. Legs flailing, she fisted one hand in his pristine button-up and jerked hard. The sound of rending material filled her with a moment of triumph before she tried to wrap her free hand around his throat. It didn't work, he was too built, too tall, too much man. Still, she yanked on his shirt to pull him close while her other hand wish-boned his neck and shoved. Honestly, she didn't know what in the hell she was doing, but Mason's grunt of disapproval had her gnashing her teeth maniacally.

Good! She wanted him hurting like he'd hurt her.

"I said leave," she shrieked, like his failure to listen was justification for her sudden attack.

But any victory she felt, any gratification she'd had, faded as fast as it had come. In one deft move, Mason spun her so fast, her stomach dipped. In a blink she was back on the couch, pressed into the cushions with Mason's big body on top of hers, her thighs on either side of his hips as he went nose-to-nose with her and snarled, "Stop!"

The command in his tone had chills blasting up her spine and something foreign pooling low in her belly.

Blinking up at him, Amanda tried one last push but was awarded with Mason letting more of his weight settle on top of her. Panting, she blinked angrily up at him while he breathed just as heavily and glowered down at her.

No one spoke. Whatever needed to be said carried between them on the electric currents of their heated stares, and when Mason's gaze dropped to Amanda's mouth, she sucked in a shuddering breath and held it. She meant to say something or do something. She meant to tell him to get off of her, to get out, but instead her heart stuttered to a halt. Mason's eyes lifted back to hers and softened, almost pleadingly so, and Amanda felt the fight leaving her. That was all it took.

Mason's mouth lowered to hers and when his lips pressed into hers, they were confusingly gently. For all the emotion they'd just expended, she'd expected ferocity, she'd expected taking. But this? This was him asking.

Breath mingling with his, Amanda slowly opened her mouth. It was all the invitation Mason needed. The passion she'd expected from him detonated like a land mine. In a flash, his hands were suddenly everywhere. His tongue slid between her lips and then he was kissing her deep, like his life depended on her. A moan wrenched its way up her throat as her arms wrapped around him. She would have been embarrassed if the sound hadn't evoked a growl from Mason that rumbled in his chest and had her arching her body to feel it more fully as it vibrated against her.

Strong hands gripped the front of her shirt and almost as if in retaliation, Mason ripped the whole front of her shirt open before he shoved the material aside and cupped a lace covered breast. Lips sucking, tongues licking, breath heaving, they feasted on each other, their hands memorizing each other.

Mason's hands left Amanda's breasts to grip her thighs where he squeezed and growled deeper. As if of their own volition, Amanda's legs lifted then crossed at the ankle behind his back. His hips rocked into hers and she had to break the kiss to gasp as the hard bar of his erection ground against her sensitive clit and had slick heat prepping her for a wanton invasion.

Mason only let her break the kiss just long enough for her to catch her breath and then he was devouring her mouth all over again. With a soft mewl that begged for more, Amanda rolled her hips and gasped hard when Mason pulled back and arched his back. The veins in his throat were standing out, throbbing hard, but that wasn't what held her captivated. It was the incisors at either side of his mouth that slowly elongated and stabbed into his full lower lip.

In her mind, she knew she was supposed to be terrified. Instead, her womb clenched and had her bucking her hips against his. She wanted those teeth closer, grazing her throat, grazing her inner thighs.

"Hey!" A male voice called from the doorway. "Everything alright in here?"

Mason untangled from her and stood so fast that Amanda could do nothing but lay there and pant.

Smoothing a hand through his disheveled hair, Mason, sniffed then dipped his chin in a nod, eyes on the door as he tried to adjust his tattered shirt. "Yes. We're fine."

The male at the door responded, "Sorry, Mr. EnemyHunter. I thought I heard an argument. A female yelling."

Mason dipped his eyes to Amanda, but she was already sitting up, one hand holding the front of her torn shirt together while the other attempted to smooth her hair into place. Standing, she kept her back to the intruder at the door as she skirted Mason and offered a breathy, "I'm fine. Everything's fine." She made her way toward the hall and her room at the end. "Thank you, gentlemen." Then by way of dismissal, "Good night to you *both*."

In her room, Amanda quietly closed the door behind her, locked it, then pressed her shoulders into it, and lifted trembling fingers to her swollen lips.

What in the hell just happened?

Chapter 16

Mason glowered at the Sentry whose nose apparently didn't fucking work. Swallowing hard, he fought the urge to cross the room and pummel the man. Instead, he pulled at the front of his shirt, straightening it as best he could before ordering, "You're dismissed, Sentry."

"Base," the Sentry offered. "My name is Base."

Mason shot the guy a look. No wonder he couldn't scent that he wasn't needed. From what Monroe had told Mason of Base, the man was human. He'd been mated to a Skin Walker female who'd been kidnapped and murdered. Base was employed at StoneCrow because he had nowhere else to go. Most humans mated to Walkers typically died if something happened to their mate, but that phenomena was more prominent with human females mated to Skin Walker males. Now, Mason felt a bite of guilt at having considered punching the poor guy.

"Mason," he clipped out and nodded his head at the man. Normally, he'd cross the room and shake hands with him, but right now, his cock was still so damn hard that it'd make walking difficult.

"You two gonna be okay?"

"Yeah," Mason shot a look down the hall. "We're fine. In fact," he heaved a weighty sigh before shooting Base a hollow smile, "I was just leaving too."

Eyes sliding back down the hall, Mason was almost certain his retreat was what Amanda wanted, but goddamn if her body hadn't said differently. Honestly, he didn't know what he'd been thinking. She'd be showing up for her first day working as his assistance in the morning, and he'd just accosted her.

Bloody hell!

So much for keeping things professional.

***

Amanda's fingers stayed on her lips, heart still hammering as she tried to calm herself. Fingers trembling, she lowered them when she heard the front door close. Straining to hear, she wondered if Mason had left too, and when silence reigned, she decided he had. Good. She didn't know what to say to him, or how to react after what had happened between them. Replaying the scene, she tried to figure out when exactly her outburst had turned to passion. Heat seared her cheeks when she thought of seeing Mason again, which, glancing at the clock, would be after what was sure to be a sleepless night.

Shoving up off the floor, she paced to the plush bed and dropped onto it, eyes scanning the room. Things had changed so much in such a short amount of time. There was no denying that the accommodations at StoneCrow manor were ten-times better than back at her cabin, but she was reluctant to enjoy the splendor of her suite. Yeah, it was out of spite, but still. Being told she had no choice about leaving still had her riled up. Riled up enough to attack Mason.

Instantly, her mind flashed back to his lips on hers, his big body settled in the cradle of her thighs. She couldn't help but wonder how far they would have gone if they hadn't been interrupted? Desire pooled low in her belly only to be quickly replaced by shame. She hadn't spoken to Remy. She hadn't officially broken it off with him yet, and she'd just made out with Mason.

Burying her face in her hands, she shook her head slowly. How had this happened? How had her life become this, this...*mess*? Just out of spite, she wanted to throw Mason's job offer in his face. But with no vehicle, she didn't have a way to get to and from the school where she'd been teaching. That got her thinking.

Shit!

Picking up the phone beside the bed, she bristled when the female receptionist asked too familiarly, "Yes, Ms. Chandler, how can I assist you?"

"Can you connect me with the Belt Valley rural school?" It was late and no one would be there, but she could at least leave a message.

"Unnecessary," the chipper voice on the line informed. "Mr. EnemyHunter has already terminated your employment with the school district."

That bit of news had Amanda squeezing the telephone tightly as she clenched her teeth and bit out an insincere, "Thanks," before she slammed the phone's handset into its housing.

Mason had dragged her here knowing she wouldn't be allowed to leave, then he'd quit her job for her! Angry tears flooded her eyes as she picked up the receiver again.

The same chipper voice answered, "Ms. Chandler?"

"Mr. EnemyHunter, please."

"Right away."

There were a few clicks and then Mason picked up. "Amanda?"

"I quit! I'm not working for you, and I'm going back to my cabin in the morning."

She hung up before he could respond and then hurried out of her room and down the hall. Rushing the front door, she engaged the bolt lock and crossed her arms before smiling smugly. It felt good to take back a small semblance of control. Honestly, she didn't know if Monroe would allow her to leave the Estate let alone go back to the cabin that *he* apparently owned. It didn't matter though. Amanda wasn't going to be bullied by anyone. She didn't need anything from anyone!

Her bravado lasted all of a minute before she was back on the phone and asking the receptionist to connect a call to Cindy KillsPrettyEnemy, and thank fuck, Cindy picked up on the second ring.

Chapter 17

"You sure you're okay out here all alone?" Cindy leaned forward in the driver's seat and eyed Amanda's darkened cabin. "Seems...spooky."

With a soft chuff of laughter Amanda reached for the door handle. "It's not spooky. This is where I live."

Reclining back in her seat, Cindy looked curiously at Amanda. "RedKnife said you were staying at the manor."

Swallowing hard, Amanda was glad for the dark interior of Cindy's Charger. "Change of plans," she clipped out, hoping Cindy didn't notice the brittle quality of her tone. Lifting her arm, she rushed on, "Once Jenny was able to heal me, it was decided that I could stay or go." She shrugged nonchalantly. "It was up to me."

Cindy's eyes narrowed to suspicious little slits. "So why, again, was your door locked from the outside? You were in such a rush to get out of the manor that I didn't really understand your explanation."

"Oh," Amanda laughed thinly. "Accident. Mason was showing me how to use the locking mechanism. We must have messed it up."

Cindy's face scrunched in confusion but before she could ask any more questions, Amanda was levering herself from the passenger seat.

"Thanks again." She turned and waved a little too wildly before reigning herself in and dropping her hand to pound up the front steps of her cabin. She fumbled with her keys under the blaring headlights of Cindy's car and, no doubt, her friend's scrutiny, until finally, the key slid into the keyhole. Halfway in the door, Amanda turned and tossed Cindy one last wave and a false grin before hurrying inside.

Back pressed into the door, Amanda panted as her heart raced. It felt like she'd escaped from Alcatraz, when, in reality, sneaking off from StoneCrow probably had more dire consequences. The triumph she'd hoped to feel was disappointingly absent. In its place was a heap of guilt and a twinge of fear. So consumed with one-upping Mason, Amanda hadn't really given much thought to what Monroe's reaction would be to her sneaking off the estate. Worse, she'd implicated an unwitting Cindy, which only lent to her guilt.

Shoving off the door, Amanda flicked on her lights and stripped out of her coat. Her boots came off next and then she quickly started a fire and then made a bee-line for the fridge.

Five minutes later, she sat cross-legged on her sofa, a fuzzy blanket covering her legs with her toes peeking out from where they were propped on the coffee table as she enjoyed a peanut butter and honey sandwich and a cold beer. Eyes intent on the fire, her body was tense from the cold that still lingered in the cabin. Though her home was small, it still took a while to get warm and right now she was blaming Mason for her cold state. He'd taken her to StoneCrow knowing that she wouldn't be allowed to leave and that pissed her off. Why wouldn't he forewarn her? At least let her pack some clothes and make preparations to her cabin. The longer she thought on it, the more upset she grew, until her sandwich sat like a lead weight in her belly. Taking her plate to the sink, she rinsed it and left it in the sink for a more thorough wash tomorrow. Right now, she was exhausted.

Snagging a second beer, Amanda cracked it on the way to her room. She was mid-chug when she shoved open her bedroom door and flicked the light on. Instantly, she froze. Eyes quickly scanning her room, nothing looked out of place, but something felt wrong.

Lowering her can of beer, Amanda slowly scoured her room, looking for anything out of place when her eyes snagged on her dresser. The top right drawer was slightly open, and she knew *she* hadn't left it like that. One of her quirks was being annoyed when drawers or cabinets weren't closed all the way.

Eyes narrowing on the drawer, Amanda slowly paced toward it, ears straining, and heartbeat picking up. At the dresser, she set her can of beer on top and slowly pulled the offending drawer open, knowing what should be inside. A sharp inhalation escaped her and her mind began to race when she found the drawer empty.

"What the fuck!" she hissed quietly.

Someone had come into her cabin, into her room, and had taken every single pair of her underwear.

Fury and embarrassment washed over her, but those emotions took second fiddle to her apprehension. Was this a joke? Had Remy been here?

Turning away from the dresser, Amanda hustled to the bathroom and turned on the light. She'd half expected to find a pile of panties tossed on the floor in the room, but to her dismay the bathroom was pristine. Rushing back to her room, she dropped to her knees and lifted the comforter to check beneath the bed. Nothing. Back on her feet, she searched the closet, and then the other drawers, but there was no sign of her underwear anywhere. For a moment, she considered that Mason may have sent someone to collect her clothes, but everything else she owned was either still hanging in the closet or folded in the dresser. Pacing, she considered calling Mason, but then he'd know she'd left the estate. But if neither Mason or Remy had stolen her unmentionables then someone else had been in her home, and in her private things. That realization had dread pitting in her stomach.

Her eyes sliced to the shotgun she kept propped against the wall next to her nightstand and when her eyes landed on the black barrel, she felt the grace of relief that was too short lived.

The sound of booted feet on the porch outside had hope and fear raging a war within her. *Please be Mason, please be Mason!*

"Hello?" she called out tremulously as the footsteps thudded slowly across the porch. With no response, she tried again, "Mason! Rem-Remy? Is that you?"

The only response was the sound of the footsteps stilling. Everything went silent aside from the rapid beating of her heart. Then a loud pounding shattered the silence as someone pounded hard on the front door.

Terrified, Amanda shouted, "I have a fucking shotgun, and I'm not afraid to use it!"

This time, there was a response, but the cold, sinister, unfamiliar laugh wasn't the reply she'd been hoping for.

Chapter 18

Heart in her throat, Amanda clutched her shotgun to her chest. Fear held her in place as the masculine maniacal laugh from the porch died down. More pounding on the door filled her cabin and fury snapped Amanda right out of her fear.

Motherfucker! This was her cabin, and she wasn't about to be bullied into terror by some stinking hillbilly or Skin Walker playing mean games.

Storming toward the front door with shotgun in hand, Amanda knew she'd make a menacing sight as she jerked the door open and snapped a rude, "What?"

A man stepped into the doorway and had Amanda's insides going cold at his appearance. Something with him was...off.

"Hi?" Amanda's tone turned soft, wooden almost as she squeezed her rifle tighter, trying to sound casual and slightly repentant. "You lost? You breakdown and need help?"

The guy was gross looking. His clothes were dirty, his dark hair was matted like it hadn't been washed in ages, and even from the distance between them, he smelled bad. Beady eyes stared at Amanda, but his expression was completely blank. No shock, no friendliness, no malice. Just a face blank as stone.

Trying not to curl her nose at the guy's stench, Amanda waited for his response as an eerie feeling pressed against her skin.

The guy's eyes darted around the room and Amanda took advantage of the opportunity to inch backward. They guy was invading her space, but that wasn't the reason she backed off. She did so because she'd need distance between them if she wanted to use the shotgun she held. She'd only backed up a step or two before the guy's attention sliced back to her, his expression going dark as he stomped one foot loudly like a petulant child, who was unhappy with something.

"Wh-what do you want?" Amanda asked more firmly doing her best to sound angry when alarm bells were blaring inside her head. Palms sweating now, heart racing, her thoughts instantly went to Mason. *Why in the hell did I leave the manor?*

The guy at the door didn't say anything, just stared at Amanda a moment before his eyes slid lower, slowly going from her eyes to her mouth, and then sliding lower still. Greedy eyes devoured her and had a shiver of repulsion sweeping over her.

"You need to leave!" she demanded.

The guy's bloodshot eyes jerked up to hers, and then slowly, almost with a casual familiarity, he stepped over the threshold as a boney hand lifted to the wooden door and tried to push it open.

"Hey!" Amanda yelled. Panicking now, she shouldered her rifle, aiming it at the man. "Get the fuck outta my house!"

With a slow shake of his head, the man tisked loudly and kept right on advancing.

Shock at his foolish audacity held Amanda still only a moment before she growled, "Last warning, asshole."

He kept right on stalking her, so with no other recourse, Amanda pulled the trigger!

A deafening click filled the room and had all the blood rushing from her face. Eyes rounding, she tried to fire again but the shotgun only clicked a second time.

The man huffed a laugh and lunged for Amanda, but she was already moving. With a speed lent by fear, she turned and raced for her bedroom. The man's booted feet pounded after her, but Amanda was already blasting through the door to her room, she shoved it so hard that it banked off the wall. She didn't care, she couldn't. She raced for the far side of the room and ran into the bathroom, quickly locking the door as she panted against it. Her relief at making it to safety lasted only a moment because two seconds later the guy was pounding on the door so hard that Amanda had to throw her body against it, afraid he'd break in.

Turning, she shoved her back against the door, pushing with all her weight as she lifted her shotgun to inspect it. She checked the safety catch and then pulled back on the bolt to extract a round, thinking the gun was jammed. With her hand covering the ejection port, Amanda tensed when it stayed empty. Quickly flipping the rifle over, she pressed the carrier latch and shoved her finger up the magazine tube.

Ffffuck!

Fear hit swift and hard when she realized someone had removed all the ammunition from her shotgun.

Amanda searched the bathroom for any form of weapon while the intruder pounded harder and harder on the door. Aside from beating the guy with a plunger, there wasn't anything useful she could use. Swallowing hard, she whimpered at how dumb she'd been to leave StoneCrow without her cell phone.

The man stopped banging long enough to laugh out, "I emptied it so you wouldn't do anything stupid."

Terror filled her at the thought of this guy being in her home without her knowledge. Eyes darting about the room, Amanda considered trying to shimmy out the tiny window high on the wall but aborted the idea just as quickly. It was far too small.

"Just come out and talk with me. This doesn't have to go badly."

Frustrated, Amanda gritted out, "What the fuck do you want?"

Silence reigned a moment before the man whispered, "My brother back." Then more loudly, "But that ain't gonna happen. So, I'll settle for who it was that made him disappear."

Shaking her head in confusion, Amanda panted a frustrated, "Wh-what? What in the hell are you talking about?"

"Them things up on the mountain," the man explained. "They're protecting her, but you can bring her to me."

"Listen, guy," Amanda tried to sound calm. "I don't know who or what you're talking about. This is my place. Mine alone. I don't know anything about any *things* up on the mountain or anything about a woman."

"Now see, you're lying to me and that's just gonna piss me off."

"I don't know what you're talking about!" Amanda screamed.

"I seen you with her. And tonight, I watched you come down from up there. So, here's what you're gonna do. You're gonna go up there and talk Lilly into coming down with you.

You're gonna keep your mouth shut about me, and you're gonna get her down here alone."

"Lilly?" Amanda breathed. "Lilly Mulholland?"

"No!" the man snapped. "Lilly Worthington."

Worthington? Amanda knew Lilly had taken King's last name when she'd recently married the Chief of Security for StoneCrow Estates. Lilly's maiden name was Worthingtonbut Amanda had no clue why this psycho would be looking for Lilly. Whatever the reason, Amanda knew King wouldn't tolerate it. An attempt on Lilly's life had already been made, and Lilly had only just recovered.

"Look, I don't know what your beef is with Lilly, but if you just let me make a phone call, I can get this squared away."

Silence again and Amanda prayed he was considering it.

"That's better," the man agreed. "That way I still have you here as collateral."

Head falling forward, it knocked into the door as Amanda prayed he meant it. "Yeah," she breathed out. "I can call and get her to come here and that way you don't have to trust me not returning or me trying to send anyone else. I'll call Lilly, get her to come here," she lied. She had zero intention of calling Lilly. The only call she'd be making was directly to Mason because she knew he'd come to her rescue. Hell, he'd been doing it ever since the incident at the bonfire, and after the kiss they shared, well, Amanda prayed it meant something more than just mere physical attraction.

"You're gonna have to open up and let me in to allow you to make that call. Because if you had a phone in there with ya, you'd already be on it." There was a sudden pounding on the door. "So open, sweet thing."

That definitely wasn't happening.

"Just slide your cell under the door," Amanda prompted looking down. "It'll fit through. There's plenty of room."

"Nah," the guy made a weird sucking sound. "I'm gonna watch you make the call, so you don't try dialing the cops."

Unable to help herself, Amanda huffed a humorless sound. This asshole was worried about the cops when there were much bigger and badder things on this mountain that he should be fearing.

They bantered for what felt like hours. Amanda trying to get the guy to trust her with his phone and him refusing. Back pressed into the door and eyes on the window, Amanda was trying to buy some time. She knew that in the morning Mason would discover her missing and then he'd surely come barreling down the mountain good and pissed to give her a piece of his mind. Right?

Pinching her eyes closed, she silently prayed, "Mason, please come find me!"

"You know what?" the guy outside her door finally heaved an explosive sigh. "You're fucking with me. And you're wasting my time. But I got ways to get you outta there. Hold tight, sweet thing."

Pressing her ear to the door, Amanda listened as his footsteps retreated. She was tempted to crack the door open and peek out but didn't. She wasn't that dumb. Ear to the door, she heard muffled noises, but couldn't make out what the guy was up to. It wasn't until she heard a strange crackling and then caught a flickering of light near the window that realization hit.

A fire! He started her cabin on fire!

Rushing to the tub, Amanda stood on the lip and peeked out the high window. Something was definitely burning, and it was definitely her cabin.

Climbing down, Amanda hurried to the door and jerked it open. She'd taken one step out before the guy was stalking toward her through the bedroom door.

"Shit!" Amanda backtracked and locked herself back in the bathroom. It was already getting hotter in the room and there was dark smoke seeping in through the wooden boards that made up the walls of the cabin.

Spinning in a quick circle as her heart raced erratically, Amanda didn't know what to do. With no recourse left, she snatched the shotgun from where she'd had it propped near the door. Bracing both feet on either side of the tub rim, she steadied herself and then smashed the butt of the gun into the small bathroom window. It took several tries before the glass finally shattered. Cold, biting air filled the bathroom, giving Amanda one second of relief before the small window started sucking in black smoke. Dropping the shotgun, Amanda gripped the edge of the window, not even noticing the searing pain of glass biting into her fingers and palms where she pulled herself up as far as she could and screamed, "Masooooon!"

Pounding at the bathroom door started and this time it was almost as frantic as Amanda's galloping heart. Gripping the windowsill harder, she kept right on screaming. "Masooon!"

Pulling herself up, she had no choice but to try and cram herself through the small window, flames growing outside be damned. It wasn't an easy feat. The window was so tall that Amanda had to use her feet against the wall to help hoist herself up. She cried out at the pain from the glass cutting her hands, but it couldn't be helped. She'd just gotten her head poked out the window when hands grabbed her from behind and jerked her back inside, her body falling hard against an unforgiving body as they both hit the floor.

Chapter 19

Mason stormed down the carpeted hallway toward his humiliation. He wasn't looking forward to the conversation he was about to have, but it couldn't be helped. This morning he'd woken up early and had called over to Lilly Mulholland to borrow some work clothes for Amanda. After retrieving the clothes, he'd stopped at the cafeteria for two coffees and then made his way up to Amanda's suite, both nervous and excited to see her. They hadn't spoken since their *encounter* the night before and reflecting on it all night, he realized just how inappropriate his actions were. He was going to be her supervisor for Christ's sake.

He'd stalled just outside her door and took a moment to force a mask of indifference that was in direct contrast to the slowly swelling erection in his slacks. Hell, just the merest hint of her scent and he was remembering her soft body pressed up against his. He'd knocked once and let himself in, only to find the suite empty. A few phone calls and he'd discovered from the operator that Amanda had called Cindy KillsPrettyEnemy. After a brief conversation with her Mason was pissed. He'd been outsmarted and he hadn't even expected it.

Now, shoving open the door to Monroe's office, Mason swallowed uncomfortably, preparing the verbal lashing he was about to endure.

Two steps into Monroe's office and Mason slammed to a halt. It took all of a second for his eyes to slide from where Monroe sat behind his desk to the Sentry standing in front of it, arms crossed, and a look of disgust on his face.

Remy bloody McCabe!

Mason was nose to nose with Remy before he even realized his own intentions. But Mason couldn't stop the rage that flooded him. He was known for his self-restraint, but right now, it took everything he had to curl his hands into white-knuckled fists and not use them. He was holding himself back. Barely. Inside, his animals surged to the fore and polluted his voice when he snarled, "Stay the fuck away from Amanda Chandler."

Mason didn't miss the sudden cloudburst of confusion in Remy's eyes before he could mask it.

Brows spearing down, Remy's voice was filled with menace when he fumed, "I go where the fuck I want, pretty boy."

Pretty boy? Admittedly, Mason wasn't a Sentry, but that didn't mean he couldn't beat seven shades of shit out of Remy.

Taking another step forward, Mason pressed his nose into Remy's as he glared at the other Walker and warned, "Stalk her again, leave her anymore *presents*, and you'll fucking answer to me."

Remy's scowl faltered before he jerked back and asked, "Presents? What in the fuck are you talking about? I've been on mission. I haven't been by her place in weeks."

Mason's adrenaline had surged at their confrontation and it had his heart beating a mile-a-minute, but at Remy's admission, Mason's mouth went dry. "The dead animal on her door, that wasn't you?"

Remy's brows furrowed, but he stayed silent. It was answer enough.

Ffffuck! Fuck, fuck, fuck! Mason's chest started to tighten. "Is Amanda in trouble?"

Ignoring Remy's question, Mason glanced down at his watch. *Shit!* She'd been home alone all night. All *fucking* night!

Turning, Mason rushed for the door while behind him, Remy demanded, "What dead animal? Is Amanda in trouble?"

Clenching his teeth against the feral possessiveness that ripped through him as Remy hurried to follow, Mason fought the urge to tell Remy to fuck off. There was a good possibility though that Amanda was in trouble, which meant Mason had to suck up his pride. "Someone's been messing with her," he snarled, quickening his pace. "We assumed it was you."

Remy bit out a terse, "*We?*"

Unwilling to explain himself and nearly to the door, Mason almost collided with the black-clad Sentry who hurried into Monroe's office.

"Crow!"

"Now what is it?" Monroe snapped shoving up from his desk.

"Fire!" The Sentry answered swiftly and pointed toward the window. "You can see the smoke from here. Bishop says it looks like it's that little cabin just down the mountain."

Mason's chest grew tighter with the dread that was filling him. Whenever he was away from Amanda he felt like he couldn't breathe right, but this... This was suffocation. This was helplessness. He knew the emotion well from all the years of searching for his sister. Barreling out of Monroe's office, he heard the Dominant barking out orders. Mason was down the grandiose central staircase of the manor and unable to control them any longer, he let his beasts take his skin just as he blasted out the main doors. He had to get to Amanda!

Chapter 20

Mason had never experienced terror like this in all his life. Heart hammering, his eyes stung from the wind as his Peregrine falcon form reached max speed. Remy had chosen cheetah form and had shot out of the estate, but Mason had lost sight of him a few miles back, and for the first time in ever, Mason prayed Remy got to Amanda before he did. With wings tucked in a full dive, Mason was topping out at speeds of near two-hundred miles an hour, but it still felt like he was flying through quicksand. Why was he going so goddamn slow!

Eyes narrowing in on the plume of smoke that was billowing up from Amanda's cabin, he couldn't help the little start of his heart when he realized it wasn't coming from the chimney.

He started praying. *Please let her be okay! Please let her be...*

A piercing scream filled the air and echoed off the mountains, turning Mason's blood to ice in his veins. She was screaming...for *him!*

Tucking his wings tighter, he made himself as aerodynamic as possible as he hurtled toward the cabin with the speed of a comet. The closer he got, he couldn't see anyone, but did make out footprints in the snow that were too large to be Amanda's.

Motherfucker!

Why? Why hadn't he forced her to stay in the guestroom in his suite? Why hadn't he just spent the night with her? She didn't need to be out here in the wilderness all alone. She needed protection. She needed *his* protection.

Another scream ripped through the air, but Mason was leveling out now. Headed straight for the cabin, he was coming in too damn fast, but it couldn't be helped. When he was just a few feet from the ground, a shift exploded through him. The paws of his mountain lion form hit the ground and he extended his claws and caught the frozen earth. The impact tugged painfully at his nails. His mountain lion's body spun wildly until his tail was facing the cabin and all his claws were tearing into the ground leaving dark gouges where rich earth was exposed. When his rump slammed into the cabin wall, Mason was already clawing for momentum to shoot himself forward. Without even considering the door, he leapt through the nearest window, his ears following the sounds of Amanda struggling. When he tore into her bedroom, the sight that met him had a massive roar exploding from his maw.

Some fuck was straddling Amanda while she was trying to fight him off. There was blood on her hands, her face, the floor, everywhere! Her shirt was ripped, but she was fighting back against the guy that had one hand wrapped around her throat and the other hand tightened in a fist that was cocked back like he was about to throw a punch. That fist disappeared when Mason lunged forward and ripped the guy's entire hand clean off with one bite.

With an agonizing howl, the fucker spun and looked at Mason.

Unlike most Skin Walkers, Mason considered himself fairly diplomatic. He wasn't easily prone to violence like most of his brethren were, but right now, seeing this prick on top of Amanda, scenting her blood...he lost it.

With a dull thud the hand in his mouth hit the floor and then Mason had his claws buried deep into the guy's flesh before ripping him off Amanda and mauling him. A mauling was the only way to describe it too. It was brutal, savage, merciless. In seconds flat, he had the guy's life snuffed out and in a rare first, Mason didn't care. There wasn't even an ounce of guilt in him for what he'd just done. No, the only thing coursing through him was a rage that was so visceral he couldn't tamp it down, not even when he spun and faced Amanda who'd scrambled backward and was staring at him with round, terrified eyes.

Holding up bloody and shaking hands, Amanda tried to placate Mason's beast with a quivering, "E-e-easy."

His eyes dipped to her bloody palms and his lip ticked up on a snarl. He wanted to kill the fucking guy all over again, only he wanted to do it slowly this time.

Forcing a shift, it felt like his skin was being peeled off. His animal wasn't convinced the danger to Amanda was gone, he was reluctant to let the man take his skin but Mason forced it. With a roar, Mason shifted and was left panting on his knees as he forced a secondary ripple over his skin. His clothing was regenerated and then he was moving.

He grabbed Amanda more firmly than he should have, but his body was still in fight mode.

"Where are you hurt?" he demanded in a voice thick with his animals.

"I'm...I'm not," Amanda began.

Mason couldn't control his fear-fueled rage. He'd almost lost her tonight. That fucking guy had hurt Amanda and would have done God knew what else to her, and it had the inky black tendrils of horrified panic wrapping around his throat and choking him.

"Where are you hurt," he thundered, his hands tightening on Amanda's biceps almost bruisingly.

"M-my hands." She held them up in front of his face. "Just my hands. I cut them on the window."

"Your face," he snarled.

"The blood dripped on me when I was trying to protect myself."

Mason clenched his teeth hard at the image her words evoked. He was acting irrationally, he knew it, but he couldn't control himself.

Releasing Amanda's arms, he scooped her up and carried her toward the door.

"M-mason?"

"We're leaving!"

Amanda didn't argue, which was good, because right now he couldn't acquiesce to her wishes, not a single one. The animals in him wanted her close, and the man in him needed her body held tightly against his, a confirmation that she was safe.

Stalking through the cabin, Mason bristled when he heard Remy shout from outside, "Amanda!"

Fuck! A partial shift shuttled through him, raising course fur all along his skin before it shrunk back inside. Wickedly long incisors punched through his gums too before they receded. Faintly, he heard the hum of motors and the whir of chopper blades telling him that the cavalry was coming, but he didn't need them. He only needed to get Amanda out of here.

Halfway through the front room of the cabin, Mason slammed to a halt when Remy raced in. Eyes jerking down to Amanda, he breathed, "Amanda!" Eyes slicing up, he frowned at Mason and held his arms out, "Give her to me."

This time when Mason's incisors pushed slowly back out, he let them. "The fuck you say," he snarled, tightening his grip on Amanda.

"Guys."

They spoke over Amanda's soft interjection.

"I said, *Give*. Her. To. Me." Remy commanded. "She's not your responsibility."

Unable to stop himself, Mason growled, "The fuck she's not!"

Amanda tried again, "Guys?"

"She's your employee," Remy countered. "That's what Crow said. Nothing more. She belongs to me."

Snarling, Mason took a challenging step closer. "You don't fucking deserve her." His voice belied his blinding possessiveness when he countered low and almost too calm, "And she's not yours. She's *mine*."

His admission had Remy jerking back, his expression blanking. "But she's…"

"Mine!" Mason repeated, this time allowing the menace that was flooding him to fill his voice. Dipping his chin, his expression was fierce as he ordered, "Move!"

***

Amanda didn't know what was happening. Mason wouldn't put her down and the longer Remy stood blocking them from leaving the cabin, the tighter Mason's hold on her grew. Remy looked just as confused as his gaze slid from Mason to her.

Mason growled, "Eyes up here, fuck lips!"

Gaze jerking up, Remy's body tensed and had Amanda wondering if the two men were going to go to blows.

"I can walk." She wiggled and pressed a hand to Mason's chest in an effort to get him to put her down. The action spread open the cut on her hand and had her hissing while jerking her hand back, and that fast they were moving.

In two long strides, Mason was to Remy and then in a move so fast he blurred, Mason lifted a foot and kicked Remy hard square in the middle of his chest. Remy flew backward out the door as Amanda gasped, but Mason didn't stop moving. Outside, all hell was breaking loose. Humvee's and blacked out trucks were surrounding her cabin. There was even a helicopter in the sky, circling her property and kicking up snow and ice so she had to bury her face in Mason's chest.

Mason hurried toward one of the Humvees and barked, "Open the door."

A black-clad Sentry did as ordered and then Mason was inside with Amanda on his lap.

"To the infirmary. Now!"

Slowly, the adrenaline from all that had happened started to dissipate and had Amanda shivering hard. Her hands burned from the cuts she'd made trying to escape through the window. Her bones ached too from where the stranger had thrown her on the ground when she'd tried to flee. Her stomach roiled with the thought of what could have happened had Mason not shown up when he did. Just the thought of that man touching her had Amanda fighting to keep from retching, which started a fit of coughing. She'd inhaled a great deal of smoke and once she started coughing it up, she couldn't seem to stop.

"Easy," Mason crooned, softly patting her back and brushing his lips against her forehead with a murmured, "I've got you. You're safe."

Sniffing back the tears that threatened to fall, Amanda pushed away from his chest just enough to blink up at him with tear-soaked eyes. "But you don't," she breathed. Swiping at her nose, she shook her head. "You don't have me, Mason."

He blinked down at her silently for long tense moments. Amanda watched so many emotions play across his handsome face but then he jerked his head away to glare out the window. Speaking low, almost as if to himself he said, "I planned to ask. In my head, when it happened, I always asked." Looking back down at her he snarled, "But apparently I'm more animal than man, and I can't chance a rejection."

His words didn't make sense. What was he...

Intense gaze focused on Amanda, Mason released her hip and reached up. His lips thinned into a grim line as he ripped the halo from where it hung around his neck. He didn't even grimace as his throat was branded with the halo's removal. Before Amanda could ask any questions or even protest, Mason thrust his hand forward. A high-pitched whine filled the air and a blinding ethereal light flashed from the halo as it locked in place around Amanda's throat.

"Mason!" But that's all she got out because her vision dimmed. The world around her tilted on its axis and regardless of how hard she fought, Amanda couldn't keep the world from collapsing inward until she was swallowed up by nothingness.

Chapter 21

Mason paced the sterile halls of the infirmary while StoneCrow's Chief of Surgery, Jenny Arkinson, tended to Amanda in one of the med rooms. King Mulholland, stood with his shoulders pressed into the white tile wall, his eyes tracking Mason as he relayed all he'd learned.

"His name is Casper Jamison. Fourty-two, attended school in town for Water Quality Management, but dropped out after the first semester. He owned a parcel of land over near Neihart." He snorted, "He's Richard Jamison's brother."

If the name was supposed to mean something to Mason, it didn't. Shooting King a glare, he scowled as he continued to pace and waited for an explanation.

On an explosive sigh, King pushed off the wall. "The guy that came after Lilly last year."

Mason stopped pacing, his head turning to King as he slowly started to piece things together.

"Casper had been on a tear ever since his brother disappeared." King lifted a hand and plowed it through his hair.

"This was about what I did to Richard. It had nothing to do with Amanda."

Mason started pacing again and only partially listened as King went into a diatribe of why killing Richard Jamison had brought his brother to the mountain seeking revenge. Mason didn't care about any of it now. Richard Jamison was dead and now so was his brother, Casper. "Any other brothers we should know about?" Mason bit out.

"No," King informed. "No other living relations. That should be the last we see of the Jamison family."

Honestly, Mason couldn't care less that he'd annihilated the last of a family line. What he did care about was how Casper had gotten so close to Amanda without anyone noticing. Because her cabin was the closest property to StoneCrow Estates, security was supposed to monitor her land. Clearly, that hadn't been done.

"I'll go over all this with Remy when he's finished his meeting with Crow. You can head up to your suite, we'll take it from here."

Mason stopped pacing and shot King a venomous look. "I'm not going anywhere! And you won't go over shit with Remy because Amanda is no longer his concern. She was never *his*! He used her as a plaything. He let danger get close. He doesn't deserve her!"

King smirked and drawled, "And you do?"

"She's mine!" Mason boomed. Heat flooded his face as his hands curled into tight fists.

"Easy," King acquiesced holding up his hands in a placating gesture. "Easy, man. I'm just making sure this isn't some fucked up power play to get back at Remy."

Mason snapped, "Get back at him for what?"

"I don't know," King sighed scrubbing a hand down his face. "I can't keep track of everyone! I don't ever know who's pissed at who or what rivalries are brewing. There are too many Walkers flooding in now. It's fucking chaos."

"This isn't a rivalry," Mason challenged. "It's a claiming." Tugging at the neck of his button-up shirt, Mason revealed the raised scar where his halo used to be. "She's mine. My mate, my one, my Angel!"

"And I get that man, but does she? She's human and from what my Lilly says, Amanda felt abandoned by Remy, which means there's a pretty good chance that she doesn't trust Walkers." He shook his head and stared at Mason sadly. "There's a good chance she might not accept you, and you need to prepare yourself because if that's the case, you need to be able to walk away."

Squaring up, Mason raged, "She's my fucking *Angel*, King. I'm not walking away. Not now, not ever!"

"Mason, man..."

"No!" Mason cut him off. "I'm not letting her give up on me, or on us."

Just then the door to Amanda's room opened and Jenny stepped out. Mason hurried to her even as her eyes slid from one man to the other in clear curiosity before she cleared her throat. "She's gonna be fine. I had to stitch the lacerations on her palms. Other than that, there's just a few bruises from being thrown around but she'll be ok."

Mason took a step toward the room, but Jenny placed a hand on his chest, halting him.

"Mason, I think Remy would like to see his Angel before anyone else does."

Vision clouding with a crimson rage, Mason's body shook as he gritted out. "She's not *his* Angel. That halo around her throat belongs to me. She's *mine!*"

Jenny's eyes dipped to his throat as her mouth fell open in silent shock. Dropping her hand, she stepped back. "I-I apologize. I just thought…"

"You thought wrong," Mason growled.

When he made to step around Jenny, King said, "Mason, I'm gonna need to question her."

Glaring over his shoulder, Mason grunted, "Not now."

"There's a dead body being disposed of as we speak. Monroe's gonna wanna know if she had any ties to him."

"She doesn't know him."

King shrugged. "Crow's gonna wanna know why you went all mauly lion on him too. We could have questioned him, turned him over to the authorities."

"Questioned him?" Mason snarled the words with clear disdain. "He was hurting her."

"I get it, I do. Hell, I delivered Lilly's attacker's heart to her on a silver fucking platter, man, but that doesn't mean it was right. I mean, we don't even know if Amanda actually knew the guy. What if they have a past. What if she..."

"Stop!" Mason thundered, turning to face King. "Amanda was attacked because *you* forgot to tie up loose ends," he spat accusingly. "You put her in danger. You're the reason she's in there hurt."

Blowing out a pent-up breath, King planted his hands on his hips and stared at Mason a moment before jerking his chin toward the door. "Go to your woman. We'll talk about this when you're head isn't so clouded with the affliction."

The affliction? That's right. So caught up in all that had happened, Mason completely forgot about the affliction. It was a reaction caused in Walker males upon the introduction to that Walker's mate, his Angel. The three part process of claiming, collaring, and binding of Amanda would have to be completed before the affliction would subside. Until then, Mason would be unable to eat, drink, or sleep. Too consumed with thoughts of coupling with their Angels, Skin Walker males were likened to rutting bull elk. Urged on by their desire to ensure only their seed is passed on, the Walker males focused solely on claiming their Angels. It was all-consuming, and Mason was already feeling the effects. Being even just mere yards away from Amanda felt too far and had his skin itching, his spine tingling with unease.

Shoving thoughts of the affliction aside, he concentrated on the only thing that mattered. Amanda! Brushing past Jenny, Mason disappeared into Amanda's room.

Chapter 22

Amanda came to feeling groggy and sore. Everything ached and it took a minute to remember why. When she did, her eyes snapped open on a startled gasp. She tried to jackknife to a sitting position, but the pain in her body prevented that from happening. All she managed was another fiercer gasp as her wide, fear-filled eyes searched the room.

In a flash, Mason was hovering over her, crooning, "Easy, love. I'm here."

His hand captured hers, but she couldn't feel his skin. Pulling her hand back and lifting it, she saw that her palm was wrapped with gauze, just the tips of her fingers were poking out of the bandage.

"What...what happened?"

"You cut yourself trying to escape."

"Is he..."

"Gone. I took care of it. He won't come after you again."

With a tremble in her tone, Amanda blinked up at Mason. "H-he was...was in my house. He..."

Sitting on the edge of the bed, Mason curled a hand around the back of Amanda's neck and pulled her into his chest. He couldn't stand the scent of her fear. It gutted him and riled his inner beasts all at once.

After long minutes of holding her while she cried softly, Amanda finally sniffed and asked, "How did I get here? Did I pass out?"

Mason swallowed hard, knowing he'd need to tell Amanda about collaring her.

"I-I remember your lion crashing through the door," she muttered almost to herself. "I remember you ripping that guy off me, and then…"

Pulling back, Mason kept his hand curled around the back of her neck as he looked at her, his thumb gently stroking her jaw line.

Eyes snapping up, Amanda's mouth fell open as she remembered everything. Slowly, she lifted her hand and her fingers grazed over the halo around her throat before she breathed a nearly inaudible, "Mason?"

She knew what the halo around her throat symbolized. She'd been friends with Cindy and Lilly long enough to be a trusted ally to Walker kind. Which meant she also knew this couldn't be real. An inexplicable panic filled her as she dropped her hand and demanded, "Take it off."

"Amanda," Mason began softly, but she wasn't having it.

"Take it off!"

She didn't want Mason like this. Not like *this*! The fear he must have felt at the prospect of losing another female who he'd grown close to would have incited him into making a rash decision. Amanda knew he felt responsible for his missing sister. She knew that the not knowing ate at him every day. He beat himself up for it. He *hated* himself for it, but Amanda knew that if he claimed her like this, he'd eventually hate them both for making that mistake.

"I want it off," she repeated, blinking back stinging tears.

"Amanda," Mason grabbed her hand, "you're freaking out. Just calm down."

But she couldn't calm down, because right now she wanted all the joy that should come with being collared by Mason, but it wasn't hers to take. And fuck! She wanted to. She wanted to throw her arms around him and kiss him long and deep before confessing her love, but this wasn't going to be her fairy tale. There'd be no happily ever after here. Not for them.

"Take it off," she pleaded. "Please!"

Instead of doing as she asked, Mason released her hand, shoved to his feet, and plowed a hand through his hair as he began pacing. "Is this because I failed to protect you?" He stopped pacing and splayed his legs wide as he frowned down at her. "Are you..." He swallowed thickly as if the words were hard to say. "Are you *rejecting* me because I failed to protect you?"

She winced at the harshness of his tone and the implication of his words. "No," she breathed. "You didn't fail to protect me, Mason, because I was never yours to protect. I..."

"So, it's Remy then," he snapped. "You still want him."

Anger sizzled through her. "No! I don't want Remy."

"But you don't want me either."

"Not like this," she blurted. When his expression darkened dangerously, she continued, "You did *this*," she gestured toward the halo, "because you're trying not to make the same mistakes you did with *her*."

Mason's eyes narrowed to cruel slits.

"I'm giving you an out, Mason." She dropped both hands on her lap as one lone tear tracked down her cheek. Tearing her eyes from his, she looked at her lap, unable to maintain eye contact and say what needed to be said. "I want you. I do. But I want you to want me too."

"I do!"

"Do you!" she raged, her head shooting up. "Because you haven't said a single thing to indicate you feel that way. Not even now. I'm sitting here wearing your halo and... I can't." She shook her head hard. "I *won't* be a replacement. I can't fill the hole that's in your heart Mason. I'll never replace your sister. And I don't want you trying to make me fill that void."

"I don't expect you to!"

"You can't just collar me and pull me close because you can't stand the prospect of losing me."

Before the argument could continue, the door burst open and Remy raced into the room. Panting hard, he looked from Mason then to Amanda before rushing for her. "Thank fucking God!"

The second Remy hauled Amanda into his arms, a pain like nothing she ever felt ripped a scream from her as she fought the embrace.

In a flash, Mason was there, jerking Remy back with a snarled, "Take your fucking hands off her."

Confused, Remy looked from Mason to Amanda and watched as she rubbed at where his skin had made contact with her arms. Eyes sliding up to the halo around her neck, he demanded, "What in the fuck is going on?" He looked from Amanda to Mason and back. "Amanda! What in the hell is going on?"

"I collared her," Mason sneered. "But don't worry. It's coming off."

Amanda's head snapped up and tear-filled eyes landed on Mason.

His eyes glittered with fury as they locked on hers. "She chose you."

Amanda shook her head slowly, her mouth falling slightly open with the intent to protest. But Remy was faster.

"Take it off now!"

"I want to." Mason tore his eyes from Amanda to glare at Remy. "But I can't do it right now. She's still healing and has just woken from the claiming. Removing it now would hurt her."

"Take it off!" Remy bellowed.

Amanda flinched, hurt that he was more concerned with who had a claim to her than the pain she'd feel. She was certain he didn't care about collaring or claiming her either. He just didn't want anyone else doing it. Remy didn't want her, he never had, but his pride wouldn't let another Walker claim her either, and in that moment as the sound of Mason and Remy arguing over her faded to background noise, she realized how very insignificant she was. Mason wanted her to fill the void left by his missing sister, and Remy wanted her because he was like a spoiled boy with a toy that he no longer favored but still didn't want to give up.

"Out."

Mason and Remy were nose-to-nose now, raging at one another in a volume so loud that neither heard her. Swallowing thickly, Amanda raised her voice and shouted. "Out!"

When both men's head whipped around to look at her, she glared at the pristine white sheet covering her legs and gritted out, "Both of you. Get out. Now!"

"Amanda," Remy began, but she jerked her head up and screamed, "Ooooout!"

Remy recoiled and looked from her to Mason. She couldn't bare to meet either man's eyes even though she felt the heavy weight of Mason's scrutiny. She knew that if she looked at him, she'd change her mind and beg him to keep her. She *wanted* to be his, but what her stupid heart didn't understand, her head fully realized. Mason didn't want an Angel. He wanted to make amends for what he felt like was a failure where his sister was concerned. He wanted to rescue a woman and be done with it. He wanted to feel that closure of saving someone. She couldn't allow it. Despite how much she wanted to be collared, claimed, and bound, she couldn't let Mason make this mistake. And a mistake is what it would be.

"What's going on?" Jenny demanded as she rushed the room. "Is everything alright?" She ignored both men and looked at Amanda who muttered, "I want to be alone."

Brows spearing down and expression going hard, Jenny turned on the men instantly. "You heard her." Lifting a hand, she jammed her finger toward the door. "Out. Both of you. Now!"

Mason was the first to move for the doorway, stopping just as he reached it to look back at Amanda.

Lifting her chin, she met his gaze and held it. Her heart squeezed at how hurt he looked, how lost he seemed. But she couldn't be what he needed. She refused to be a simple replacement for something precious he'd lost. She wanted to be his one, all consuming, not just some consolation prize. So, as difficult as it was, she ripped her gaze from his and ignored Remy as he approached the bed and lifted a hand to touch her, stilling his fingers just an inch from her face as she recoiled.

"I'll be back, baby," Remy promised, and the words soured her stomach. She wasn't his baby. She wasn't Remy McCabe's anything, but that admission would have to wait. Right now, she just wanted to be alone. Exhaustion was plaguing her, and the pain from Remy's touch was still throbbing through her, making her feel edgy and anxious.

"Did you hear me?" Remy prodded.

Head snapping up, she couldn't keep the bitterness from her voice as she bit out. "Leave." Feeling bad at the wounded look he gave her, she tagged on a reluctant, "Please. Just leave."

She didn't have to be a Walker with heightened senses to know Remy was angry. His expression said it all when his lips thinned and his eyes narrowed to cruel slits as he shot daggers at Mason's retreating back. Remy followed Mason into the hall before Jenny closed the door, sealing the two women in the finally quiet room. The silence lasted a fraction of a moment before she heard Remy and Mason arguing in the hall. She knew it wouldn't be over between them. She knew they'd most likely even come to blows, but that wasn't her problem right now. Right now, she had to figure out what she was going to do.

Chapter 23

As soon as they were alone in the hall, Mason turned and grabbed Remy by the lapels of his Sentry uniform before shoving him hard against the wall. "Touch her again, while she's wearing my halo and I'll fucking end you. Got it?"

Remy's fist came up before Mason could anticipate it. Mason's head snapped to the side with the impact as Remy snarled, "I'll touch her whenever the fuck I want. She's mine."

Slowly, turning his head back to face Remy, the two men were nose-to-nose for only a brief moment before all hell broke loose. Fists flew, and enraged as he was, it was easy for Mason to get the upper hand. Remy had not only touched what Mason considered his, he'd hurt Amanda by doing so. Just remembering her pain-filled scream fueled his rage and lent him a strength only borne to a Walker defending his Angel. It took all of his strength not to shift and let his beasts tear Remy apart, but as good of a pounding as he was giving Remy, it was all too brief. King and Bishop raced down the hall and separated the men. Glaring at

Mason, Remy turned his head to the side and spit blood from his mouth. "This isn't over!"

"You're bloody right, it's not," Mason countered. He didn't care what Amanda said, her scent didn't lie. She'd wanted him the night before, just as much as he'd wanted her, and she hadn't lied when she'd spoken to him about breaking it off with Remy. What he didn't know is why she was balking now. Yeah, he'd failed to keep her safe, but she couldn't truly fault him for that. He'd secured her at the estate. *She'd* been the one to sneak off.

Should have been smarter, his inner-self sneered. He knew Amanda wouldn't just tolerate being forced into anything. He should have known she'd devise a plan. He should have prepared better, but even if he had, there'd been no accounting for Casper Jamison. That whole thing had come from left field and no Walker could be faulted for missing it. ...well, maybe King *should* be faulted. He should have done better follow-up after killing Casper's brother, tied up all the loose ends, but Mason got it. Right now, even with Casper's body still cooling somewhere on the Estate, Mason was fully consumed with only one thing. Amanda. She could have died tonight. She would have if he hadn't gone racing to her rescue. Hell, even now, her cabin and belongings were nothing but ash still smoldering on the ground. Just thinking of how her delicate body could have been among the carnage, had his animals clawing at his insides. His beasts wanted Mason to turn around and storm back into the exam room. They wanted to claim Amanda and keep her, and fuck it'd be so easy to do right now. She was in a fragile state and Mason knew he could persuade her into letting him take her, but he wouldn't. Because she wanted his halo off and that meant there was something in him that she found lacking. Instantly, his thoughts went to his failed search for his sister. Did Amanda think he couldn't keep her safe because he'd failed to do so with his sister? Did she think he was a failure because he still hadn't found her? The possibility soured his stomach and had him feeling a combination of both shame and self-loathing on a scale he'd never experienced.

Bishop led Remy down the hallway while King ushered Mason toward a door at the other end of the hallway.

"Give her a minute," King suggested quietly. "Amanda's been through a lot in the last twenty-four hours."

Mason shot King a withering look that he'd hoped would silence the Sentry, but no such luck.

"When my Lilly was hurt, she had a lot to process. And in the end, she chose me."

And that had Mason's gut twisting because he didn't think he stood a chance with Amanda, so in proper male fashion he took out his anger on the closest person. "You should have done your homework. Amanda could have died because of your failure to secure all the loose ends of your actions."

"You think I don't see that?" King snapped. "That fuck came here looking to hurt my Lilly. I know better than anyone else how this could have ended. But you have my word. No other relations of Richard Jamison will be coming around."

Mason shot King a doubtful look, but the Chief of Security crossed his arms over his chest and lifted his chin. "I did the follow-up I should have done the first time. There are no relations or friends of Richard Jamison's left. This trouble is finished."

"Your trouble," Mason snorted, shooting a look back down the hall.

***

Inside the exam room, Amanda angled her face away from where Jenny stood watching her silently near the door as war raged on the other side and then fell silent.

"You okay," Jenny asked.

Not wanting to cry in front of the Chief of Surgery, Amanda tried to make her voice light, but it came out sounding brittle when she murmured quietly. "I'm good. You should go check on them."

"Amanda." Jenny was across the room and sitting on the edge of the bed in a flash.

Amanda's attention stayed on the door where there was loud yelling in the hall. "Seriously. Go check on them. Someone might be hurt."

Lips thinning into a grim line, Jenny shot a look of displeasure toward the door. "They're grown men. They'll figure it out." Her attention went back to Amanda and she reached for one of Amanda's hands but stalled. "I'd hold your hand, but I don't know if I can. I'm still learning about all the facets of the affliction."

"I'm not afflicted, Jenny."

"No," she corrected quietly. "But Mason is."

That had Amanda shaking her head dejectedly. "He's not. I'm not his. He just," she gestured toward the halo, "put this on me because he's trying to make up for not finding his sister."

Jenny shook her head, her lips pursing a moment before explaining, "That's not how it works. He doesn't get to just pick some random woman to fill a void."

"Well that's what happened." And Amanda didn't want to talk about it now. In fact, she didn't want to talk about it again ever. Fisting the halo, she asked, "Can you take this thing off."

Sadly, Jenny shook her head. "Only the Walker gifting his halo is able to remove it."

"Then get him back here," Amanda choked out. "I want it off."

"How 'bout we get you healed first? Your Walker's halo will help speed that process."

"He's *not* my Walker."

"Remy then."

"He's not my Walker either," Amanda fumed feeling stupid tears beginning to fill her eyes.

"Hey," Jenny consoled. "It's gonna be alright. One thing at a time, okay. First you heal, then we deal with the love triangle."

Snorting a delicate sound, Amanda sucked back her tears. "There is no love triangle, Jenny, because there's no love. Mason doesn't love me. He loves the idea of me. He loves the thought that I can fill that hole that he's drilled into his own heart. And Remy." She shook her head sadly. "He never loved me. Not now, not when he was lying in my bed. Never. I'm just... I'm unlovable."

"Stop it," Jenny hissed. "You're not unlovable, Amanda. You're just upset, confused, exhausted, and injured." Jenny stood and went to a drawer. She came back with a syringe that she shot into the IV going into Amanda's arm.

Amanda watched her administer the medication. "What's that?"

"It'll help you get some rest."

"I don't want to rest," Amanda argued.

"Yeah," Jenny pushed gently on one of Amanda's shoulders, being careful to keep from touching her skin directly as she eased Amanda back on the bed. "But you *need* to rest."

"What I need is to get the hell out of here." Amanda wanted to argue more, but the drugs worked too quickly. She swore one minute she was mid-blink, and then there was nothing.

Chapter 24

Amanda stood in Monroe StoneCrow's office for the second time in less than a week feeling like a naughty child being brought before the principal. Fidgeting, she wavered under the Dominant's intense scrutiny. She'd woken early feeling groggy, but still attempted to sneak out of the infirmary without anyone noticing. No such luck. Jenny had caught her in the hall and had forced her back to the exam room to check her hands and to run a few tests. King showed up shortly after and once Amanda had been cleared by Jenny, King had escorted her to Monroe's office.

"So, you're not Remy's." He stated simply.

Amanda didn't respond, so Monroe narrowed his eyes on her. "Then you're Mason's?"

Her response was instant. "No. I belong to no one."

"That halo around your throat..."

"Was a mistake," she cut in, tired of the game. "Look, I'm not here to discuss my lov..."

Clearing her throat, she started again. "I'm not here to discuss my *affairs*. I'm here because I want to leave the estate, and no one can seem to make that simple request happen." She shot a dark look over her shoulder at where King stood by the door, arms crossed over his chest with a smirk on his smug face.

"And where is it you think you're going?"

Monroe's tone irked her almost as much as the way he phrased the question.

Turning back to him, she groused, "I don't *think* I'm going anywhere. I *am* getting dropped off in town as soon as we're finished with whatever this is."

Monroe leaned forward, fingers lacing over the top of his desk. "And then what?"

Amanda blinked back at him in response.

"You've no home to return to, no clothes or personal effects to retrieve, they are all ash. And you have no money to secure a temporary place. So, what's the plan?"

"I have money," Amanda countered sourly, knowing that the cash she'd pulled to fix her truck was all her savings.

Pursing his lips in a show of impatience, Monroe eased back in his seat. "You have a minimal amount of cash, no vehicle, and let's be honest, no other real option other than staying here until you can get on your feet."

"I don't *want* to stay here!"

"Well," splaying his hands in front of himself in a show of helplessness, Monroe shrugged. "It can't be helped now, can it? Which is fine. We don't mind hosting you."

Asshole! Of course, it could be helped, and him pretending to be powerless was so outlandish that she rolled her eyes. "If you're so interested in helping me, then you can give me a loan." Turning, Amanda was headed for the door, knowing even before she looked up at King and his sad expression that she wasn't going anywhere.

"This isn't what I wanted when I assigned Remy to you, Amanda."

She froze, Monroe's words swirling around in her head on a mocking loop. *"...assigned Remy to you, assigned Remy to you, assigned Remy to you."* Slowly, she turned, not bothering to fight back the ill feeling that was constricting her chest and had bile rising in her belly. "What?" she whispered. *Assigned?*

Assigned! All the air left her on a whoosh as Monroe's words slowly sunk it. *Assigned him to me?* She repeated the words out loud as tears flooded her eyes. "Assigned him to me?" She cast an accusatory glance at Monroe, but she couldn't hold eye contact as embarrassment and humiliation washed over her. Everything inside of her went cold. She and Remy had met when he'd "stumbled" upon her cabin. He'd been the one to introduce her to StoneCrow and its inhabitants. He'd been the one to bring her into the Skin Walker fold.

"This was a setup from the beginning?" she accused. "You..." She felt heat stain her cheeks as she raged, "Was him bedding me part of the plan too?"

Monroe had the decency to look shocked. "No. That's not what happened. I..."

"No!" she snarled cutting him off. "Enough. Enough of your shit! And enough of this place." Turning again, she rushed the door and when King made to block her, she shouted, "Move out of the way before I scream."

Yeah, she'd been played, but she had friends at StoneCrow now, and one of those friends included King's Angel, Lilly, which meant King wouldn't go man-handling Amanda without facing backlash from his mate and they both knew it.

"Amanda," King began, but the door was shoved open behind him.

"Took you long enough," Monroe snarked as Mason entered.

Mason's gaze instantly went to Amanda and stayed on her. "What's wrong?" He was on her in three long strides, his hands cupping her cheeks and titling her head up so he could inspect her face. "Why are you crying? What happened?"

"Nothing!" she tried to jerk out of his grasp and back away from him, but Mason only pulled her closer, one arm circling her waist to hold her to him as he turned and glared at Monroe. "What did you do?"

"Bought you time," Monroe bit out in a bored tone. "You're welcome, now take your Angel and get your house right."

Amanda was glaring at Monroe now right along with Mason, but at the word Angel, she jerked back from Mason. "I'm not his Angel." Reaching up, she fisted the halo hanging around her throat. "This thing is coming off and then I'm going."

Mason's attention slid back to Amanda. He took a step toward her, but she retreated just as quickly. "Going where?"

"Nowhere!" Remy answered as he strode into the office.

A quiet, "Jesus Christ" exploded from King before he placed himself between Mason and Remy and looked to Monroe for guidance.

"Enough," Monroe bit out tersely. "Ms. Chandler, I've been patient up to this point..."

"Patient?" she screeched. "All due respect, but there isn't a patient bone in your body, Mr. StoneCrow!"

"You're right." He shoved up from his desk and the look of displeasure on his face had Amanda falling silent, wondering if she'd gone too far.

Pleasantries gone; Monroe turned matter of fact. "You're not leaving, Amanda. You know too much about us for us to let you go just now. You're staying for as long as it takes for *me* to believe I can trust you. But in the interim, I can't have this," he waved a hand toward her, Mason, and Remy, "disrupting my Estate. You'll need to choose."

Confused, she shook her head. "Choose what?"

From between clenched teeth that warned of Monroe's rapidly fading patience he gritted out, "Between them." Jerking his chin toward Mason and Remy, his narrowed gaze slid back to her. "Now."

Amanda stumbled back a step and breathed out, "Wh-what?"

"It's that or a cell," Monroe informed.

Mason crossed to stand protectively in front of Amanda, a growl rumbling its way up his throat.

Monroe shook his head, "And I don't want to have to do that to you." Shifting his gaze, his eyes narrowed pointedly on Mason. "But I don't have the resources to afford you an escort right now. We're stretched thin, and the only way to keep an eye on you is through your Walker or by locking you up."

"My Walker? Lock me up?" she squeaked the latter.

With a slow inhalation, Monroe shifted his eyes to Remy and then Mason. "One of you will oversee Ms. Chandler. I don't care which it is, Amanda, but you need to choose between them or a cell." He glanced down at his watch, "And you need to do it now. I'm busy."

Amanda, who'd been cowering behind Mason's massive frame, backed away from him. "I'm not..."

"You are," Monroe bit out tersely, "And you're choosing now, or I'm choosing for you."

Chapter 25

Mason was pissed. Monroe was pushing Amanda too hard. He wasn't giving her the time or the space she needed, and it had Mason fighting the urge to challenge the Dominant. His patience was tested further when Remy stepped forward and cleared his throat.

"She's already chosen me."

"The fuck she has!" Mason snarled, hanging on by a mere fucking thread.

"We're together!" Remy boasted. "We have been." Brows spearing down, he glared hard at Mason. "Where did you even come from? Why you sniffing around my girl?"

Mason opened his mouth to respond, but Amanda stepped out from behind him. "I'm not your girl! I'm no one's girl, and I won't be choosing anything or anyone." Her gaze shifted to Monroe. "Not now, not ever."

Monroe shrugged. "So, a cell then. Fine." He looked to King who'd been leaned up against the wall, arms crossed, one leg bent with his booted foot pressed into the wall, waiting.

At Monroe's glance, King inhaled sharply, a look of disapproval on his features as his gaze slid from Monroe to Amanda.

"So that's it!" Amanda snapped. "Pick Mason, Remy, or imprisonment?"

Monroe shrugged negligently as if what he was forcing on her wasn't a life changing moment.

The room fell silent, and when King lowered his arms and stepped away from the wall, Mason stepped forward, possessiveness nearly blinding him. "Touch her and you fucking die!"

Remy stepped forward too but instead of confronting King, he faced Mason. "No one's touching her. Not King, and especially not *you*," he sneered.

Amanda tore her gaze from Mason and glared at Monroe. "Lock me up."

Monroe didn't even blink as he drawled, "King."

King glared at Monroe too. "You expect me to fight them both."

"You're the Chief of Security," Monroe reminded. "Call your men."

"Stop!" Mason demanded, lifting both hands to stay any action. "I have a solution."

All eyes turned to him, but his gaze swept to Amanda. "You say you don't want either of us, so prove it."

Confusion knitted her delicate brows.

Taking a step closer, he challenged, "Prove it, Amanda."

Frowning hard, Amanda bit out a terse, "And how exactly do you suggest I do that?"

"Kiss me."

His words had her frown slipping.

"Wh-what?"

"Kiss me," he goaded, stone-faced. "You want to prove to me that you don't want me the way I want you, then kiss me and show me that I don't affect you."

***

Kiss him? She couldn't. She *wouldn't*. "That's ridiculous," Amanda spat, but was already shaking from the prospect. Heat slowly started to pool in her lower belly, and, as if she could tame it, Amanda settled a shaky hand over her abdomen.

"Why?" Mason stalked toward her. "If it won't matter, then show them. Show *me*, Amanda."

She tried to retreat when he advanced the one last step that put him brushing up against her, but her legs refused to listen. Perhaps because her brain was too busy trying to find a way out of the situation. "That wouldn't prove anything."

"Actually," Monroe cut in, his eyes narrowing on her. "It would." His nostrils flared and his eyes narrowed even further. "Hell, her scent is changing just at the prospect."

Startled, Amanda turned her head to the side and sniffed at herself. She didn't smell anything, but when she looked at Remy and saw the look of anger clouding his features she knew that, coupled with his silence, was proof enough.

"I'm s-scared," she stated.

"Nah," King shook his head. "You are scared, but that ain't got shit to do with the scent you're emitting."

Again, Amanda sniffed at herself. Still nothing. Glancing up at Mason's intent expression, she squeaked, "R-Remy?" When she looked to Remy for aid, he remained silent, his face a mask of hurt and confusion.

"It's just one kiss," Monroe goaded. "What could it hurt?"

But Amanda knew what it would mean. Hell, if they could already scent her excitement, her anticipation, she knew it would only grow stronger if she were wrapped up in Mason's arms, his mouth on hers.

Without a word, Mason reached out and wrapped his arms around her waist. Before she could protest and just as Remy growled, "Stop!" Mason pulled her in and then his mouth crashed down on hers.

Dazed at first, Amanda remained stiff, but that didn't last long. The scent of Mason did something to her head, the heat from his body melded hers into a pliancy. His lips were soft on hers, persuasive and not forceful like she'd expected. When his tongue swiped against her lips seeking entrance, she complied and then all bets were off.

Before Amanda knew what was happening, her arms were lifting and wrapping around Mason's neck. The scent of him, the feel of him, made her lightheaded. He felt safe, he felt like home. Distantly, she heard what sounded like a roar, but she was too absorbed in Mason's kiss to care. Eyes closed, she returned Mason's kiss with an urgency she'd never experienced before. Not only did she want Mason, she *needed* him, and it was that need that frightened her. For a long time, she'd believed that she needed Remy too, but to him she was just a convenience. To Remy she was a plaything, something he toyed with when he was bored. Never once had he gifted her his halo or ever even mentioned doing so. Mason on the other hand, hadn't hesitated. He'd collared her and now he was asking to claim her.

You're just a filler to him too, her mind whispered. *When he finds his sister, he'll regret choosing you.*

She tried to break the kiss, but Mason snarled against her mouth and pulled her closer. The hard bar of his erection pressing into her belly silenced her mind. He wanted her too.

Whimpering, Amanda gave up the fight. She kissed Mason back with wild abandon until he finally broke the kiss.

Forehead pressed into hers, he panted, "You're mine, Amanda."

Wrapped in his embrace, trying to catch her breath, Amanda nodded against his forehead.

"You're fucking dead!"

The enraged snarl had Amanda's eyes snapping open. She'd forgotten about their audience. She'd forgotten about Remy. Looking over, she saw King and Monroe holding Remy back. Remy's enraged gaze was locked on Mason. "How fucking dare you!"

"How fucking dare *you*!" Mason shot back. "You left her out there unprotected and alone. If she were yours, that never would have happened."

"She was mine!" Remy snarled and lurched forward. Amanda flinched into Mason's embrace a fear-filled gasp leaving her as Monroe and King held Remy back.

Mason pulled Amanda more firmly into the safety of his embrace.

"She's chosen," Monroe thundered releasing Remy and stepping back to straighten his tie. "You're dismissed Sentry McCabe."

Remy's head whipped around to look at Monroe in shock.

"You heard me," the Dominant declared, jerking his chin toward the door. "Leave us."

Remy's hate-filled gaze sliced back to Mason and when it slid down to Amanda, she shivered at the loathing she read in his eyes. Mason pulled her behind him, blocking her from Remy's view to thunder, "Look at my Angel like that again and I'll be claiming a mate's right to battle."

"Mason!" King chastised.

It was obvious King felt bad for the humiliation Remy was suffering, but Amanda couldn't relate. Mason was right. Remy shouldn't have left her alone all the time. He shouldn't have come and gone only when it pleased him. It was obvious he wasn't her mate. Right now, he was just a little boy who regretted tossing out a favored plaything that had been picked up by someone more grateful.

Amanda didn't see Remy jerk out of King's grip, but she did hear his sneered, "This isn't over."

"No," Mason bit out, "it's not. But it will be. She's been claimed and collared. Tonight, she'll be bound, and once that's done, you *will* stay the fuck away from what's mine."

Remy's response was a deep growl as he stormed from Monroe's office. "It won't be over then either. This'll never be done."

The office fell silent as Remy departed and it stayed quiet for long minutes until Monroe finally heaved an explosive sigh. "All that and before lunch no less."

Mason turned to Amanda and pulled her into his arms, kissing the top of her head with a muttered, "Thank you, love."

His words had her tensing.

"Thank you?"

Pulling back, he looked down at her and growled, "Don't." Lifting both hands, he cupped her face. "Stop overthinking everything and just feel."

Closing her eyes, she clenched her jaw to keep her tears back. She didn't know if she was capable of what he was asking, no matter how deeply she wanted it.

"I thanked you for not making me kill him."

Opening her eyes, Amanda blinked up at him. "Kill him?"

Expression gone serious; his tone was solemn. "I would have had to in order to keep you. I'd do anything for you."

Closing her eyes again, Amanda let his words sink in. Lifting her hands, she covered his and swallowed hard, wanting to believe his words but still too heart-shy to truly trust. "Mason," she began quietly, but he immediately cut her off.

"No," dropping his hands, forced her to lower hers too. In a flash, he grabbed one hand, lacing his fingers with hers as he muttered, "Not here. We'll talk at home."

"Home?"

His gaze bore into her as he explained, "My home. *Our* home. You're staying with me."

Mason made for the door, tugging Amanda along behind him. He said nothing to Monroe or King, and it was evident by his urgency that he wanted out of their presence. It had another thought sparking to life. Had Mason just done her a favor to keep Monroe from throwing her in a cell as he'd warned? Maybe Mason had kissed her because he knew the reaction he'd evoke and that would get both Monroe and Remy to acquiesce. Well…Monroe at least. Hurrying to keep up with Mason's pace, Amanda gripped the arm that held her hand and once they were in the hall, she offered a brittle, "Your debt is paid."

Mason slammed to a halt so fast that Amanda would have crashed into him if he hadn't spun and caught her.

Brows spearing down, Mason asked, "What debt?"

"I know you've felt like you owed me something because of what you did to my arm, but…"

"Is that what you think this is?"

"Yes. *No!* I don't know."

Mason made an angry sound deep in his throat as his expression went hard. "None of this was about assuaging my guilt, love."

The tingling sensation of hope fluttered to life in her chest.

"I meant every single word of what I said in there, and once I get you to my suite, I'm going to prove it." Turning, he hurried down the hall, pulling Amanda along with him as a little yelp left her.

"Holy shit!" she breathed. Nervousness, anticipation, and anxiety started a brawl right in her belly, and she didn't know whether to laugh or to cry. She knew Mason chose the former because she could just make out the swell of his cheek.

"Wh-where are we going," she stammered.

"I told you. Home."

He said the word with such finality that it did something funny to her insides.

Home? A home with him? A home with him as hers? Was this really happening?

Chapter 26

For the first time in since he could remember, excitement roiled in Mason's stomach. He'd declared his intentions for Amanda in a room full of people, including her, and she hadn't refused him. To him, that was as good as an 'I do', which meant that right now, his incisors were throbbing in his gums almost as hard as his cock was throbbing in his slacks.

Is this really happening? Am I about to claim my Angel?

A fine sheen of sweat broke out on his forehead as his pulse began to roar in his veins.

Ffffuck!

He hadn't felt this eager, this giddy since he was a mere pup. Behind him Amanda stayed quiet and he was grateful for it. The possessiveness that had ripped through him earlier at the prospect of King even attempting to touch Amanda to throw her in a cell still had fight pulsing through him, only now it was mingled was something else. Hope? Pride? Fear? He wanted Amanda. He wanted her like he wanted his next fucking breath, but he was worried that if he gave her the chance to speak, she'd denounce his claim. It's why he just pulled her quickly along behind him.

Because his suite was just one level down, he bypassed the elevator and opted for the stairs. He was forced to slow his pace to ensure Amanda didn't stumble and even the thought of that had him spinning with a snarl. In a blindingly fast move, he lifted Amanda into his arms and then he was double-timing it. She let out a little squeak when he lifted her but other than that, it was all the sound she made. He wanted to look at her to gauge her expression, but he was afraid to. He was acting rash, he knew, but he couldn't help it. It was the nature of his beasts to aggressively battle any other male who attempted to via for a female his inner animals had already claimed. And claim Amanda he had. He was unsure of when it happened, but it didn't matter. It was done. Now, he just had to worry about if his current behavior was frightening her. When he'd gifted her his halo, the affliction had struck and struck hard. Unable to eat, drink, or even sleep, his mind was too preoccupied with fully binding Amanda to him. It was all consuming like elk during the rut. They too would forego eating, sleeping, and drinking to protect their harem to ensure only their seed, the *strongest* seed, was passed on.

At his door, he used the hand beneath Amanda's knees to open the door. It was unlocked. It was always unlocked. Walkers didn't steal from each other and they had nothing to hide.

Stepping into his suite, he used a foot to kick the door closed behind him. Amanda looked around the front room and kitchen curiously, but now wasn't the time for a tour. Mason carried her straight into his bedroom and tossed her onto the bed with an ordered, "Strip." He went at his own clothes like a man possessed and had shucked his shoes and removed his shirt before he realized Amanda wasn't moving.

Hands stilling on the clasp of his slacks, he lifted his head, his gaze boring into her. "Undress."

She didn't move.

***

Amanda had wanted to protest Mason carrying her down the stairs and hallway. She'd wanted to tell Mason to put her down and explain to him that she was a grown ass woman and could walk on her accord, but he was acting so...so...feral. When she'd

glanced up at his profile, she had to quickly look away. His jaw

had been set, his expression tight. It was almost as if he were in

pain. Perhaps he was. Cindy had mentioned something to her

about how it hurt wolf shifters to touch their mates until they

completed the mating. Something about it being mother nature's

way of ensuring that the males didn't overlook their "one." She

didn't know if it was the same for Walkers and didn't want to ask,

instead remaining silent until now. Dropped on Mason's bed,

she'd heard his command but could only watch as he ripped off his

clothing. It was a hell of a sight. The man was all golden skin and

lean muscle that flexed and bunched with his movements. He was

mesmerizing. So much so, that she nearly lost all train of thought.

Almost.

"What..." She licked her lips, her eyes on his clenching

abs, and tried again. "What are we doing?"

"We're cementing our bond, love."

His voice was deceivingly calm but looking at him told

another tale. His typically green eyes were blown out, his pupils devouring all color, and as he spoke, Amanda could see the wicked incisors he possessed poking out from beneath his top lip. He was barely in control, and she got it. With every fiber of her being, she wanted to follow Mason's command and strip bare before lying flat and offering herself to him heart and soul. But she'd been hurt too badly already by a Walker she'd had feelings for, a Walker she'd trusted. Still, even knowing how poorly Remy had treated her, she couldn't stop the guilt that assailed her.

"I hurt Remy…"

"Don't!" he snarled, his voice a rough growl. "You owe him nothing. *He* should have done better by you. We're done talking about him. For good. Now get undressed, love, or would you like me to do it for you?"

His look grew so predatory that it was almost scary. She imagined it would have been terrifying to anyone else, but she knew Mason. He'd never hurt her. Not intentionally.

He moved so fast he blurred, and before Amanda could even guess at his intentions, he had her pinned to the bed, his big body settled between her thighs and her wrists manacled by his hands. Nose-to-nose, she held only a moment before righteous indignation flared to life. Gritting her teeth, she bucked and struggled to free herself. It was a joke. Not only was Mason three times her size and a thousand times stronger, all her bucking and writhing only succeeding in settling him more firmly in the cradle of her thighs where the hard bar of his arousal that strained his slacks pressed firmly against her sex. The more she struggled the more friction against her sensitive clit had her womb aching with need, her pussy weeping in preparation.

Fffffuck! he snarled, his eyes closing tight. Mason lifted his chin and Amanda could see the veins standing out on his neck. The gravelly sound of his voice unleashed something molten low in her belly and she knew…she just knew, he was hanging on by a mere thread.

When he finally lowered his chin and opened his eyes, they flashed gold with his inner beasts. It was erotic as hell. He was a monster wrapped in finery, a lethal killing machine that was staring at her so hopefully, so adoringly that it broke her heart because as much as she wanted him, she wouldn't accept him

using her just to fill a void. It wouldn't be fair to either of them.

"We need to talk about your sister."

Her words had a confused frown claiming his features.

"I can't..." she began but then amended, "I *won't* be a

filler. If this, if *us,* is about you trying to use me to compensate for

what you're missing, what you're really wanting, it'll never work.

I can't do that, Mason. I'm not her."

Chapter 27

Mason held Amanda captive beneath him. His strong hands had her delicate wrists pinned beside her head and both of their breathing was ragged. Eyes locked on each other; he was literally salivating to taste every inch of her. But he wouldn't. Not like this. She had to want him just as much as he wanted her. Brows dipping down, he rolled onto his back and pulled her on top of him.

"I'm not in the habit of keeping that which doesn't want to be kept, love. If you don't want this, don't want us, then you're free to leave. I won't stop you."

Amanda blinked at him in surprise. "R-really?"

"Really." Letting his hands fall to his sides. He held her gaze. You're not a captive. And I won't force you to stay against your will. You've gotta want this too."

His eyes lowered to watch her pull her bottom lip between even teeth, other than that, she didn't move. Her legs were straddling him, she could climb off and walk at any second, and Mason's heart was beating a million-miles-a-minute at the prospect of losing her. It would gut him. Nah, it'd do more than that. He'd always thought the hole in his heart where his sister's love should be was the most painful wound he'd ever be forced to endure, but the prospect of Amanda leaving him had him realizing how much power she held. She could end him. And she would if she walked. He wouldn't be able to recover from the loss of her and he knew it. Still, he clenched his teeth to keep from begging. He wouldn't do that to Amanda. He loved her too much to force her to stay out of pity or guilt.

"I don't want an Angel I have to take. I want one who will *give* herself to me. I want her...*you* to want my touch as much as I need yours. Us, *this*, has nothing to do with my sister. Yes, I feel guilty about her being out in the world alone. Yes, I feel helpless, and there'll always be an empty spot in my heart waiting for her to claim, but the rest of my heart, the rest of me is yours, Amanda. I'm in love with you. I'm consumed with you. I want you as my Angel. But I want you to want that too."

***

His words rocked her to her core. His heart was hers? He was in love with her too? How had this happened? This had all started with him twisting her arm at the bonfire and then him tracking her down out of guilt and now look where they were. It felt surreal.

"Choose," he interrupted her thoughts. "If you don't want me," he shifted his gaze to the door. "Go, but go now before I change my mind and fucking devour every inch of you."

A shiver swept over her. She held the control? She got to choose?

Blinking down at him, Amanda drew in a deep breath. She was terrified of making the wrong decision, but this felt nothing like how her life had been with Remy. Remy had never once spoken of the future or of wanting her as his Angel. Remy had never loved her. Honestly, she thought she'd loved him, but now, feeling how she felt about Mason, she realized she hadn't known what love was until Mason had come into her life.

Swallowing hard, she chose to leap. "I choose you, Mason EnemyHunter. I want you as mine. I want to keep you, and I want you to keep me."

A slow grin split his face before his hands found her hips. In a blink she was on her back again as Mason rolled them and then climbed from the bed. Confused, Amanda raised up onto her elbows to stare at him questioningly. A devilish gleam lit Mason's eyes and then he reached for her foot. He undressed Amanda frustratingly slowly. He took his time unlacing each shoe and peeling off each sock before kissing the top of each foot. Then he was at the hem of her shirt, helping her lift it over her head, the long fall of her hair tangling in it a moment before falling around her shoulders. Instead of removing her bra, Mason pushed her back onto the bed and cupped her jaw, tracing his thumb along her lower lip before slowly gliding his calloused hand down her throat, between the valley of her breast, and over her quaking stomach. At the button on her jeans, he lifted his eyes to her and warned, "Last chance. If you don't stop me now, there won't be another chance, love. If I take you now, I take you forever and you me."

Unable to speak, Amanda jerked her chin down in a simple nod of agreement. She knew if she spoke her voice would tremble and she'd most likely embarrass herself by begging him to stop talking and hurry the hell up.

With a wicked grin, Mason flicked open the button on her jeans and then lowered his head to use his teeth to pull the zipper down. It had Amanda panting hard. As excitement filled her, she buried her hands in his hair and blew out a slow pent-up breath.

Was this what it felt like to be wanted, to be cherished? When he started shimming her jeans over her hips and down her thighs, she answered her own question. *Hell yes!*

She hadn't realized Mason had removed her panties with her jeans until he glided his hands up her thighs and then around her hips to cup her ass. Amanda inhaled sharply, and unwilling to go any slower, she quickly removed her bra and tossed it to the floor.

Naked on the bed, she shivered when Mason sat up onto his heels. His eyes slowly slid from hers to caress every inch of her body before he breathed, "Fucking beautiful." Standing he stripped the rest of his clothes off, and Amanda watched in awe. She knew his cock would be huge because of his size, but the hard rod that bobbed and seeped precum looked almost impossible for her to take.

As if reading her mind, he smirked and muttered, "It'll fit. Don't worry, love."

Then his hands were on her knees and spreading her thighs. She was already wet, already prepared.

Mason's eyes were on her sex, his jaw clenching before he growled, "There are a million and one things that I wanna do to you, but it'll all have to wait." Crawling up the bed, his mouth found hers and he kissed her deeply before pulling back and holding her gaze with his. He watched her as the blunt tip of his cock probed her entrance. "I'll try to go slow." Then he was slowly sinking into her.

His size had Amanda tensing.

"Relax," he commanded.

She did her best, but it was hard. His mouth lowered to her neck where he raked his teeth against her skin. The action had

Amanda inhaling sharply before a throaty moan left her. Mason pulled back and then eased back in. He did this over and over until he was fully seated inside of her, and when he was, he paused to press his forehead into hers and exhale slowly like he was trying to stay in control.

"You ready?" he asked, but his voice was polluted with his animals and almost unintelligible. It had chills blasting up Amanda's arms.

"Y-yes," she stammered as she bucked her hips.

In a flash, Mason's hands were on her hips, holding her still. He dipped his dick in and out, his hips moving sensually slow. Almost too slow. He was being gentle like he was afraid he'd break her. Hell, maybe he could. Amanda buried her face in his neck and enjoyed the feel of his skin beneath her palms, his body rocking between her thighs. She nipped and sucked at his skin and it evoked a throaty growl from Mason, but he kept his pace steady, fucking her slow like he didn't want to rush it. She didn't want to either. She wanted to stay in the moment forever, she wanted to savor every second of his claiming.

"I'm not going to be able to control myself much longer," he growled against the sensitive spot just below her ear. His words had goosebumps erupting on her flesh. She didn't want him in control. She wanted him feral. Clenching her channel, she bucked her hips again and this time she was rewarded with a growl as Mason got to his knees. His voice rough, he snarled, "I tried. But I can't wait."

Hands gripping her hips, he lifted her ass off the bed and then he was pounding into her. The width of him brushed against nerves inside Amanda's pussy that had never been touched before. It was sensory overload and almost tipped her over the edge. She had to fight not to come.

"I'm gonna come so deep and so hard inside your tight pussy…"

His words had more of her honey coating his cock.

"Mason," she panted, her breasts bouncing with each powerful thrust of his hips. Mason bucked into her with wild abandon and before she could fight it off, climax ripped through her. "Mason!" she bellowed, but he kept shuttling into her, his face a mask of concentration. "Say it," he demanded.

Amanda didn't know what he wanted to hear so she said the first thing that came to mind. "I-I love you!"

Mason's incisors elongated and poked into his bottom lip as his body grew tense. "Again," he grunted.

"I love you. I love you, Mason."

Teeth gnashed, his face gone feral, Mason bucked into her once then twice and then hissed, "Fffffffffuck!"

His cock erupted deep inside her, bathing her womb and setting off a second orgasm for Amanda that had her clinging to him, her nails raking his shoulders as she cried out again.

With one last thrust, Mason snarled, "Mine!" And Amanda felt his ownership all the way down to her soul. It was done. Collared, claimed, and bound, she was now a Skin Walker Angel.

Chapter 28

Amanda sat on the edge of Mason's desk. Straightening her blouse, she beamed as she turned her head and found Mason studying her, one arm propped on his desk, his forest green eyes alight with satisfaction. Her cheeks flushed at what they'd just done on his desk. She'd never made love in an office before and certainly never to her boss. Granted this boss was her mate, it still felt naughty and taboo.

Mason made a show of licking his lips. "Best lunch I've ever had."

Amanda blushed harder as Mason mumbled something.

"What is that?" she asked, leaning closer to him. He didn't hesitate to pull her off the desk and onto his lap where he cradled her and peppered her face with kisses like she was the most precious thing in the world.

"Every time we're done…. you know, you whisper something under your breath that I can never quite make out."

Pulling back from his sensual assault, Mason grinned. Lifting a hand, he curled it around the back of her neck before he pulled her in for another kiss. After, he breathed against her lips, "Lucky." Easing her back, he explained, "The word you hear me say all the time is lucky. I do it to remind myself how goddamn lucky I am that you chose me. How lucky I am to call you mine." He paused a moment then sighed contentedly. "Just how lucky I am, my love." He pulled her in again to press another affectionate kiss to her forehead. "Lucky," he breathed quietly against her skin.

Beaming with pride that he'd chosen her too, Amanda swallowed against the emotion clogging her throat. She was happy. God, how long had it been since she'd been genuinely happy? And it was all because of Mason. Yeah, they still needed to find his sister, and they'd always have the issue of Remy to deal with, but she wasn't worried about any of it because she knew they'd endure together!

Settling against his chest, she lifted a hand and let her fingers stroke the stubble on his jaw as a happy sigh left her. "I'm the lucky one."

"Nah," he disagreed. "Loving you is as easy as breathing. Now me on the other hand…" He didn't finish.

His words made her heart ache as her grin slipped. She knew he wondered why he and his sister had been abandoned and she wondered if he considered himself unlovable. She knew he did, but that was ok. Her job now was to prove his ass wrong, and that's exactly what she intended on doing. Smile reclaiming her face, she said the one thing that always seemed to settle his uncertainty and self-deprecation.

"I love you, Mason. I love you so damn much and I'd be so lost without you."

"You'll never have to worry about that, love. Not ever."

His vow made her heart squeeze. He didn't know it, but she'd started her own work on hunting his sister down. She wanted to be the one to give him that. She wanted to show him that she trusted that she wasn't heart filler and for as long as it took, she'd never stop trying to find Mason's sister. He deserved that closure, he deserved that happiness, but until she could make that happen, she be right there with him. Day in and day out, she'd be by his side fighting, working, fucking, loving. She was his and he was hers, and goddamn if it wasn't the most beautiful thing she'd ever experienced.

His tone was somber, just like it always was when he responded, "I love you too, Amanda. I love you more than I've ever loved anything or anyone."

He said the words without hesitation and without falsehood. It had her smile growing as she slapped his chest. "You suppose we should actually try to get some work done today?"

When she looked up at him, he captured her chin and pulled her lips close. "Why? Work'll be there tomorrow." His lips found hers as butterflies erupted in her middle, and she knew that *this* was the life God had intended for her. She'd never take Mason for granted, she'd never stop being grateful, and she'd never stop working to keep their mating a happy one.

Epilogue

Monroe reclined back in his chair, the dark leather creaking under his weight as the Dominant steepled his fingers in front of him, pressing his index fingers into his lips a moment. Silence hung in the air a moment and the only movement was Monroe's eyes narrowing to suspicious slits as he studied the Sentry standing at attention in front of his desk.

With a heaving sigh, Monroe dropped his hands and offered a single word. "Denied."

That had Remy slipping from his stance as his eyes dipped to Monroe. "Denied? Why?"

With a smirk, Monroe shook his head slowly. "I know what you're doing, and it's only going to cause trouble."

"Volunteering for an already existing mission is going to cause trouble?"

Brows spearing down, Monroe leaned forward, planting his elbows on the desk that separated him from Remy. "Don't do that," he snapped. "Don't step into my fucking office and think for one second that I don't know what in the hell is going on."

Staring at Monroe a moment, Remy blinked and snapped back to attention, his gaze going to the far wall.

"You think Mason took something that was yours," Monroe explained. "You're now wanting to do the same to him. But it won't happen. Not now. Not on my watch, and certainly not while you're under my employ. The answer isn't just no, Sentry McCabe. It's a hell no."

***

Jaw clenched tight, Remy struggled to hold back the retort that was burning in the back of his throat.

"You're dismissed," Monroe clipped out. Reclining back in his seat, his hand snatched a file from his desktop and flipped it open before he bowed his head to study its contents.

Studying Monroe's bent head, Remy considered all his arguments, all his excuses for wanting the assignment, but knew none of them would hold weight. Monroe knew exactly why Remy wanted in on the mission and denying it would not only fill the room with the scent of a lie, but it'd have Monroe questioning

Remy's worth. Sentries didn't lie to their Commander and Skin Walkers sure as shit didn't lie to the Dominant.

With military precision, Remy turned and then marched to the door, his ire rising with each step. Monroe didn't get it. No one did. Not even Mason could know the damage he'd done to Remy's reputation when he'd claimed Amanda.

Motherfucker! He'd made Remy the current laughingstock of the Estate.

In the hall, Remy closed the door behind him and strode determinedly down the long corridor regretting having even asked for permission. He shouldn't have. He should have just reported to Commander Conn Drago and been placed on a team. He should have usurped the Dominant by leaving him out of it. Now, he'd have to defy a direct order. And that's exactly what he intended to do because if anyone found Mason's long-lost sister, it was going to be him. He had every intention of finding the woman and it wasn't to play hero or to make Mason look bad. No, Remy wanted to get to her first because then no other Walker would have the chance to claim her and claiming her was his mission. He was going to take Mason's sister and make her his because Mason deserved to know how it felt. He deserved to have something precious taken from him the way he'd taken Amanda from Remy. And there'd be no guilt, no second-guessing. The instant Remy found Mason's missing sister, he was going to collar her and hide her until she agreed to be his, Monroe *and* Mason be damned. Remy wouldn't rest until he had Mason's sister in his possession, in his bed, and bound with his halo even if it meant abandoning his position on the Estate. Even if it meant going rogue.

Printed in Great Britain
by Amazon